# Taming Riki

## Volume II: A World Divided
### Part 3

# Taming Riki

## Volume II: A World Divided
### Part 3

By Kira Takenouchi

PEGASUS
HOUSE

Naples, Florida, USA

ISBN-13: 978-0-9979025-3-2
ISBN-10: 0997902531

Pegasushousebooks.com

For more of Kira's fiction visit her site at Patreon at
patreon.com/kiratakenouchi

For Rieko Yoshihara
*For Her Vision*

And

For
Camry, Coriander, Jay, Amber,
Bastet, Ginny, and Ilya
*My Blondie Premium Luxury Elites*

And

For Astrid,
*To Whom I Intend to Leave an Empire*

## Chapter 1 –

## Masters and Pets

THE BLOOD DRAINED FROM Voshka's face. "That's impossible," he said. "Anori crashed his vessel on Amoi. That's how he died."

"I'm only telling you that we've identified the craft, and it's definitely your brother's. It's moving out of its original position, on a fast course toward the Forbidden Region on Amoi."

"What was its original position?"

"We first picked up the signal at Minas Qentu. Now the craft is heading toward the Kattahar Mountains."

"That's Federation territory," Voshka noted, realizing that this was the very area Iason had reportedly been held hostage.

Very few things surprised the Commander. He was, by nature, suspicious, and so not easily conned. But this was one of those moments where he realized he had definitely been lied to, by someone.

And he had not even known it, until now.

"Thank you, Anders," he nodded.

"Should we send vessels to intercept the craft?"

"Not at this time," the Commander instructed.

"Yes, Sir."

Voshka continued on to his room, puzzling over this new information. Why was Anori's craft still functional? And why was it just now coming online, after over ten years? Hadn't it been completely destroyed in the crash? Or had the Amoians kept it, and were just now restoring it to operating status?

The Commander frowned. Another thought was looming in his mind, one he disliked very much. And the thought was this: what if Anori's ship had never crashed at all? What if he had been lied to about his death, for some reason?

He again thought of Iason's predicament on Amoi, and the questions Raoul had asked him about Alphazenian cloaking technology.

At that point he suddenly knew, without a doubt—Raoul, at any rate, *knew* about Anori's ship. And hadn't Raoul been Anori's lover?

Something wasn't adding up, but he couldn't quite figure out what it was.

He opened the door to his bedchambers, finding Aranshu still asleep on his bed. At this point, he was so distracted, he didn't even mind.

He went over to his computer terminal and decided to put a call out to Iason Mink again, once again using an encrypted Independent frequency. He could find out what the situation was from the Blondies who had his phone, and maybe get some questions answered.

He was surprised, however, when Iason answered the call from his own terminal.

"Iason," Voshka exclaimed. "I thought you were being held hostage."

"I was," Lord Mink sighed. "But Riki and I escaped."

"And how did you manage that, might I ask?"

"It was really Riki. He found an old concealed Federation exit in the dungeon where we were being kept. All I did was break the chains that were holding us."

"Oh, is that all?" Voshka teased. "Have you told your friends? They were quite worried about you."

"No, we just returned home not long ago."

"I see. So, your friends didn't arrive in an Alphazenian craft to rescue you?"

"What?" Iason replied, blinking.

"You do know what I'm referring to, I think? An old Alphazenian craft? It just went online there on Amoi."

Iason was silent for a moment. "I don't know anything about it."

"Oh? You wouldn't lie to me, would you, my friend?"

Lord Mink looked visibly startled. Suddenly Riki pushed into the screen. "Is that Vosh? Hey, Commander, it's me, Riki."

"Hello, Riki. Please excuse me if I don't seem as friendly as usual. I have a lot on my mind."

"Okay, be that way. You just need a good fuck, probably," the mongrel suggested.

"Riki," Iason hissed.

Voshka smiled indulgently. "He's right. Perhaps I do."

"Well, I'm going now, so you can talk to Iason," Riki announced, immediately disappearing from the screen.

"Voshka, about the ship," Iason began, looking uncertain.

"Yes?"

"I don't know how to tell you this."

"That sounds promising, at least. Go on."

"There *is* an Alphazenian ship here on Amoi. Your brother's ship, in fact."

"Yes, I know. What I want to know is *why* it's there, when I was told he crashed over the Kattahar mountains twenty years ago?"

Iason paused for a moment, lowering his gaze. "In fact, your brother didn't crash. That's not how he died."

"No? Why was I lied to?" Voshka asked, trying to keep his temper under control.

"Because we feared there might be a military response if you knew the truth."

The Commander swallowed hard at this, leaning forward in his chair. "And what *is* the truth, Iason?"

Lord Mink took a deep breath. "The truth is, your brother was assassinated while staying in my home."

Voshka heard these words with great difficulty. His brother had been murdered! And all this time he had thought it had only been an accident!

"And you hid this from me, all this time?" he asked, teeth clenched.

"We felt we had to. Alpha Zen is so powerful, and Amoi, well, we're nothing compared to you. We didn't know how you would respond."

"And the assassin? Did you deal with him?"

"I'm afraid he got away with it," Iason answered.

"You're telling me my brother was murdered *in your home* and whoever did it got away without any punishment whatsoever?"

Lord Mink couldn't bear to return Voshka's gaze. "Yes," he whispered.

The Commander stared at him for a long moment, then sighed, sinking back into his chair. "Iason. I thought we were friends."

"We *are* friends," Iason said quickly.

"Yet you hid this from me."

"I've told you now."

"That's true. You *have* told me. But I wonder if you ever would have said anything, if I hadn't confronted you about the Alphazenian vessel."

Lord Mink remained silent, unsure of what to say.

"Your friend Raoul knew about this," Voshka accused.

Iason looked surprised. "Why do you say that?"

"Because when I called earlier tonight and your friends were in an uproar over you, Raoul asked me about the cloaking technology of Alphazenian vessels."

"He did?"

"Yes, he did. He was quite rude, actually, as I recall."

"Please forgive him. He was probably rather distraught. And you know he *did* love your brother."

"That's what puzzles me. He knew about this, and you knew about it. The two of you. And who else?"

"Jupiter knew."

"Why did you keep the ship?" Voshka asked.

Iason shook his head. "It wasn't a matter of keeping it. The situation was more like this: we simply didn't know what to do with it. We hid it. I can't imagine how anyone found it."

"And yet they did."

"So it seems."

"So, Raoul and Anori were lovers. Could the assassin have been a jealous lover?"

"Possibly," Lord Mink agreed, trying to keep his expression neutral.

"What lovers did Raoul have then?" Voshka demanded.

"We looked into all that thoroughly at the time," Iason assured him quickly. "All I can tell you is, we never did come to any definite conclusion on the matter."

"Well, *I* haven't looked into it," Voshka snapped.

Iason was silent. He couldn't remember the Commander ever talking to him in that tone of voice before.

"I'm sorry, Iason. I'm feeling a little angry at the moment. Perhaps we should talk at another time."

Lord Mink bowed his head. "As you wish."

The Commander ended the transmission, staring at the rotating logo on his screen for a moment.

"What was that about?" Aranshu asked from the bed.

Voshka turned, surprised. "So. You're finally awake."

"How long did I sleep?"

"A long time. All day, in fact."

"Was that a Blondie you were talking to? Lord Mink?"

"It's none of your concern."

"He's very handsome," Aranshu said.

"Yes, he is," Voshka agreed.

"But what were you talking to him about? Anori? I thought your brother was dead."

"He *is* dead."

"But I heard you say he was assassinated. I thought he crashed—"

"Aranshu, hold your tongue," Voshka said sharply.

Aranshu held up his hands as if surrendering. "Sorry. I thought maybe you wanted to talk about it."

"Well, I do *not*."

"Yeah, I get that."

The Commander sighed, running a hand through his hair. "Forgive me. I'm…not myself tonight."

"So I see."

Voshka turned and regarded him for a moment. "You'll have to get used to Velo, you know. A lot has changed since you were last here."

The Aristian bristled at this, saying nothing.

"Aranshu," the Commander said in a warning voice.

"I *heard* you," Aranshu snapped.

"Don't use that tone with me."

Aranshu sighed, falling back on the bed. He immediately regretted this move, wincing when his punished flesh met the mattress.

"I see you're feeling the effects of your punishment," Voshka noted with a nod. "Good. Perhaps you'll think twice before smarting off to me again in public."

"Yes, Master."

"What was that?" Voshka prodded, delighted.

"I said, '*Yes, Master.*'"

"Well. It's quite a treat to hear you say it for once without my asking you to address me so."

Aranshu rolled onto his side, propping himself up on one arm. "Master," he purred, "can you *please* get rid of Velo? Send him back to the harem."

Voshka's lip quivered as he tried to restrain an instinctive smile. "Aren't we being sweet and cooperative now? What, you're calling me 'Master' again? But what did I just tell you about Velo?"

"I know what you said, but I was hoping it could just be the two of us, from here on out," Aranshu pleaded.

The Commander regarded him for a moment, enjoying his pet's new attitude. "I'm afraid that's not possible. Velo has been…very loyal to me for ten years now. It wouldn't be right to suddenly discard him on your return."

"He's been your pet that long?" Jealous, Aranshu pouted, looking away.

Voshka reached over and took hold of his chin, turning his head. "Look at me."

Reluctantly, Aranshu returned his gaze, but his eyes brimmed with tears and anger.

"You brought this on yourself, Aranshu. Isn't that right? You're the one who ran away."

"You know why I did," Aranshu said accusingly. "Anyone else would have done the same thing, if they were me."

The Commander looked as though he wanted to say something, but then changed his mind. He let go of his chin. "We're not having this discussion again," he said wearily.

"What discussion?"

"The one you're trying to have."

"You mean the one about my mother?"

Voshka sighed. "Aranshu, stop. I mean it."

Aranshu scowled for a moment and then decided to change tactics. He reached out and touched the Commander's arm, letting his finger glide down his uniform. "Why don't you take this off?"

Voshka looked at him, a slight smile at his lips. "Why should I do that?"

Aranshu frowned. "Don't you want something?"

"I might. Since you interrupted my congress with Velo."

"That was horrible, you making me watch. You know I hate it."

"I know you do. It was part of your punishment."

"Is my punishment over?"

"I haven't decided," Voshka answered. "It depends, in part, on your behavior."

Aranshu struggled with his feelings. On the one hand, he wanted to sulk; but on the other, he was anxious to secure his Master's affections again.

But there was another matter that was interfering with his plans. His ass was killing him. He moaned, rubbing his hand over his pant bottoms.

The Commander followed his gaze. "You're really feeling that, aren't you?"

"Yes," Aranshu whimpered.

"Let's take a look, then. Take off your pants."

"What are you going to do?" Aranshu asked, frowning.

"I just told you, didn't I? I'm going to examine you."

"You promise you won't hurt me?"

"Pet, take off your pants."

With some reluctance, the Aristian complied, pulling down his pants with great difficulty and wincing the whole while.

"Now, turn over. On your belly."

Aranshu obeyed, looking back meekly over his shoulder. "Is it bad?"

"Oh, yes," Voshka answered, rising and going over to one of his cupboards. "You need some attention. I have a special cream I'll rub into your skin; it will help with the pain and accelerate your healing."

"Will it hurt?" Aranshu asked suspiciously.

"I just told you; it will help with the pain."

"Okay, then. I guess that's all right."

"I'm not asking you, Aranshu. I'm *telling* you what I'm going to do," Voshka clarified, obtaining the wanted cream and returning to the bed. "Now, just relax. Don't clench your buttocks muscles. I'm going to spread this on you."

Aranshu was quiet as his Master administered the medicated cream. Voshka's hands were warm and the cream, while stinging initially, seemed to work instantly, relieving some of the pain.

"Ahhhh," he sighed, unable to help himself.

"Does that feel good?"

"Yeah," Aranshu admitted. "Put some of it on my cock."

"We'll use a different cream for that," Voshka answered with a smile. He reached for a tube of lubricant that was on his bed shelf and squeezed a generous portion onto his hand.

Aranshu's cock bounced in eager anticipation. "Put it on," he begged.

"If I do, can you restrain yourself?"

"Yes, of course. I'm not a—ohhhhhhh!" Aranshu moaned as Voshka began applying the sensual lubricant, instinctively thrusting into his hand.

The Commander pulled away, giving him a mock scolding look. "What happened to all your grand restraint?"

"It felt really good," the Aristian replied defensively.

Voshka laughed, unbuttoning his uniform and discarding it. Next he took off his boots as Aranshu watched.

"You said you had something for me," Aranshu said suddenly.

"What?"

"On the ship. You said there was a present waiting for me."

Voshka laughed softly. "Do you really think I'd reward you after the way you've acted today?"

"I *did* come back," Aranshu protested.

"Oh? I thought you came back to kill me," the Commander reminded him.

Aranshu looked down. "I wouldn't have *really* gone through with it."

"No? And why should I believe you?"

The young man met his gaze. "Because I missed you awfully. I thought about you…every day. I was just angry. That's why I left. But that doesn't mean I don't have…feelings for you."

Voshka, now completely naked, crawled toward him. "Ten years is a long time, Aranshu. You could have come back long before."

"I wanted to. I did. But I was…proud."

The Commander reached out and touched Aranshu's face, sighing. "Oh, Shu. You have no idea how much you hurt me."

"I'm sorry I hurt you. I had a lot of issues when I left. In fact, there's something I should tell you."

"Hmmm?"

"Something I did. Something bad," Aranshu said. "I was very angry, and I wanted my revenge.

"Are you talking about the recent Aristian massacre?"

Aranshu looked shocked. "How did you know?"

"I pieced it together. You were angry at the royal family, am I right?"

"The prince didn't do anything when you razed my village," Aranshu said hotly. "He treated you like you were an honored guest."

"So, you got your blood vengeance. Did it make you feel better?" the Commander asked.

Aranshu shook his head. "Actually, no. I regretted it. I still have…nightmares about it."

Voshka opened his arms and Aranshu snuggled up to him, sighing.

"Killing others is never easy," Voshka whispered.

"I find it interesting to hear *you* say that."

"I'm not without a heart, you know. I may be a military commander, but that doesn't mean I don't value human life."

"How do *you* deal with it? All the people you've killed, I mean?"

"I don't think about it," Voshka answered honestly. "If I did, I couldn't continue what I do."

"*Komiat?*"

The Commander smiled. "Yes, Aranshu?"

"I came back to you because I love you."

Voshka sat up on one elbow, looking down into Aranshu's eyes. "Do you really mean that?"

"Yes. I wouldn't lie about that."

"Oh, Shu," the Commander breathed, bending down to kiss him. "I've waited so long to hear you say that."

"I forgive you, for what happened to my village…and to my mother. I know you didn't want it to happen."

"No, I didn't mean for it to happen," Voshka agreed. "I was very angry about it, at the time."

"*Komiat?*"

"Yes?"

"Why did you keep me? You let all the other boys go."

Voshka smiled. "I suppose because I didn't think you were from Aristia. It was your blond hair. You were so beautiful, I had to have you."

"But you have so many boys in your harem. Why me?"

"Because," the Commander said, tracing a finger down Aranshu's chest to his nipple, "you please me. I don't know if I can entirely explain it."

"Does Velo please you as much as me?"

"He pleases me in a different way."

Aranshu pouted at this. "You must think a lot of him. I saw what you gave him tonight. And he has his own rooms."

"Is that what's troubling you? Perhaps, if you're good tonight, I'll bend and give you your surprise, after all."

Aranshu brightened at this. "You will? What's my surprise?"

Voshka laughed. "You'll have to wait and see. But first, you have to please me."

Smiling, Aranshu kissed his Master, first tentatively and then with increasing passion. "What do you want?"

"I want *you*, body, heart and soul," Voshka answered.

"You'll have it," Aranshu answered.

LORD SAMI GROANED. "My head is killing me," he complained.

"Mine, too," Heiku agreed.

"I think we're all a little hung over," Omaki said, eliciting nods of agreement from the other Blondies.

Now that the sedative had finally worn off, Raoul was feeling as bad as the others, though he remembered little of his experience while under the effects of the Laughing Gas Nitrizenaphene the previous night. "Are you sure Iason got away?" he demanded.

"We told you already a hundred times," Lord Ghan sighed. "We captured Amon Qentu but Iason and Riki were already gone by the time we arrived."

"Let's call him at home and make sure he's all right," Lord Am insisted. "He should be there by now, if you're right."

Konami shook his head. "Iason has been through enough. He's probably asleep. Let him contact us when he's ready."

Lord Quiahtenon nodded his agreement. "He's probably traumatized. Give him some time to recover."

"I still can't believe you gave Amon to Yutaku Iman," Raoul grumbled, looking at Lord Sung. "You should have given him to *me*."

"*You* would have killed him," Konami said.

"I would have tortured him first," Lord Am clarified. "Which he richly deserves, as you well know."

"Be that as it may, I had a better use for him. Yutaku has been deviant for far too long when it comes to his views on pet ownership. Taming Amon will force him to put on Master's gloves."

Raoul shook his head. "I still don't understand. After everything he did to Iason?"

"Yutaku seemed…taken by Amon. I can put it no other way. I've never seen him show any interest in owning a pet, so I thought this was the perfect answer to curb his deviance."

"You're saying he was attracted to that beast?" Raoul demanded.

Lord Sung shrugged. "It appeared that way to me. It's not all that surprising. Amon is, technically, a handsome specimen. Yutaku didn't see what happened to Iason, so he hadn't formed any preconceptions about the man."

"How can a notorious Federation Rebel be a pet? Surely you don't think Jupiter will approve?" Lord Am pressed.

"If I hear from Jupiter, I will, of course, obey according to her wishes. But until I do, Amon will stay with Yutaku."

Raoul sighed. "You do beat all, Sung."

Aertis, who had been watching this exchange, snickered a little at Raoul addressing the Headmaster simply as "Sung".

"You find something amusing about all this, do you, Aertis?" Raoul asked.

Aertis immediately grew somber. "Oh, no, Lord Am. Not at all. I just…enjoy watching all you great Blondies talking to one another in such a frank fashion, like you're all good friends or something."

"Hmmmph," Raoul muttered, though he was visibly flattered at being called a "great Blondie".

"Megala, you're awfully quiet," Omaki remarked. "And you have an extremely guilty look on your face."

Everyone turned to look at Megala, who reddened upon being the center of attention.

"So, what exactly did you do to Raoul while we were gone?" Xian asked pointedly.

"What? Me? Why, nothing!" Lord Chi insisted.

"Then why is your face so red?" Lord Sami demanded.

"What are you talking about?" Raoul asked.

Omaki turned to Lord Am. "Megala offered to stay behind and watch over you while you were incapacitated by that sedative. Do you really remember nothing that happened while we were gone?"

Raoul turned to Megala, regarding him suspiciously. "You wouldn't dare," he whispered.

"I didn't! I swear!"

"Did you take pictures, Chi-chi?" Omaki asked, winking.

"No, of course not!" Megala cried, confused. "I didn't have a camera."

This admission generated a loud reaction from everyone, except, of course, Raoul. Megala, realizing his error, looked fearfully at the great Blondie.

"Now I am going to kill you," Lord Am said calmly, before suddenly lunging from his chair and putting his hands around Megala's throat.

"Raoul!" Lord Sung seized Raoul's wrists, trying to get him to release Megala.

"You're choking him!" Heiku yelled. "Let go, Raoul!"

The other Blondies all leapt up and, together, managed to pull Raoul off Lord Chi.

The injured Blondie fell to the ground, unconscious.

Heiku knelt beside Megala, taking his vitals with a swipe of his bionic hand, which contained a built-in Series 6700 Vitalmeter unit, making him the envy of every physician in Tanagura.

"Is he all right?" Omaki asked.

"Goodness, Raoul, you almost *did* kill him," Lord Quiahtenon scolded.

"I had every right," Raoul stated, arms crossed on his chest. "He violated me."

"You don't know that," Omaki said quickly. "Jupiter's sake, Raoul, we were only teasing you!"

Lord Am frowned. "How do I know I wasn't violated? You all know what a pervert he is! You saw how guilty he looked!"

The Blondies were all silent at this, considering.

Megala's eyes fluttered opened. "What happened?" he whispered hoarsely.

"Don't try to talk," Heiku advised. "You're going to be sore for a while."

"I had every right," Raoul repeated.

At that moment, an incoming call came in from Iason Mink.

"It's Iason!" Omaki announced, running to his terminal to accept the call. "Iason? Is it really you? Where are you?"

"I'm home," Lord Mink replied. "Can't you read my terminal signature?"

"Well, yes, but—oh, we have your handheld, by the way. I'll drop it by tomorrow. Unless you're coming back to the party? We're all here at my place. Come over!"

Lord Mink rolled his eyes. Only Omaki Ghan would even consider continuing with a party after what had just taken place. "No, I think we've had enough excitement for one night," he said wryly.

"It was a good party, though, up until the point Riki got abducted and everyone got shot, wouldn't you say?" Omaki insisted.

"It was a very good party," Iason said politely.

"We went searching for you, you know. We even had Jupiter's permission. Raoul did it—he howled at the sky and Jupiter heard him, and Raoul got to talk to her. We went to rescue you, you see. But by the time we got there, you were already gone. Er—just a minute—Raoul is demanding to talk to you. He—"

"Iason!" Raoul shouted, finally shoving Omaki aside and coming onto the screen. "Are you hurt?"

"No, Raoul. I'm not hurt. That is, the ordeal wasn't pleasant, but I'm essentially unharmed."

"Thank Jupiter! I nearly went out of my mind with worry! They—that is, *we*—captured that scoundrel Amon. But you'll never guess what Konami did with him!"

Iason shook his head. "I'm sure I don't know."

"He gave him to Yutaku Iman as a *pet*! That's too good for him, don't you think, after what he did to you?"

"Why would he give Amon to Yutaku Iman?" Iason wondered aloud, completely confused.

"Oh, Yutaku was with them when they tried to rescue you. I mean, when *we* tried to rescue you. I wish Sung had given him to *me* as a pet! I would have relished that! I would have disciplined him every day of his life!"

"I'm sure that's why he *didn't* give him to you," Iason answered. "But about your rescue attempt—you didn't happen to use Anori's ship, did you?"

"How did you guess?" Lord Am asked, looking astonished.

"Because it triggered some kind of identification alarm on the Commander's security system," Lord Mink explained. "They know it's Anori's ship."

"Blast," Raoul said, looking rather pale.

"Yes, Voshka just contacted me. I'm afraid he wasn't very happy about being lied to."

"What did you tell him?"

"I had to tell him something. So I told him part of the truth— that Anori had been assassinated and that we were afraid to tell him for fear of how he might react."

"How did he take that?"

"Not well. He said he was angry and ended the call."

"That's not good," Raoul said, seeming worried.

"No, it's not."

"But at least you're safe. That's all that really matters right now."

"Raoul, how are the others? Katze, Odi, Ayuda, Askel?"

Raoul grew grave. "They're alive. But they are all in serious condition. They're at Tanagura Hospital now."

"What does Heiku say? Will they recover?"

Raoul nodded. "He says yes, most likely. But you'll need to hire new bodyguards for now."

"Where is my attendant, Toma?"

"He's at the hospital, I believe. I'm not sure whether you were aware, but it seems he had developed some sort of relationship with Ayuda."

Iason nodded. "I was aware of it. I didn't see the harm."

"Shall I send you my attendant? Yui can take care of your needs until Toma returns."

"I don't want to deprive you of your attendant," Iason protested.

"Nonsense. It would be no trouble whatsoever. He's very capable. He drove them all to the hospital, you know. I'll contact him and have him come over right away. You need to have someone to attend to you, goodness, after what you've been through!"

"Well, if you're sure it wouldn't be inconvenient."

"It wouldn't be the least bit inconvenient. In fact, I'm pleased I can do something. I was so worried about you, Iason. You know he—Amon—sent footage of what he was doing to you. We could hardly bear to watch. I nearly went out of my mind. I—"

"Raoul, forgive me. I'd rather not relive it, if you don't mind."

"Oh, of course. I'm sorry. I wasn't thinking straight. I—they shot me with a sedative and I'm still not quite myself, you see."

"I understand. But I'm…rather tired, and I have a headache. So, I think I'll get some rest."

"Yes, get some rest. Do that. I'll send Yui as soon as I can reach him."

"Have him come directly into the penthouse. I may be in bed. Entry code Mink-Goldstar."

"Mink-Goldstar. Got it."

"Thank you, Raoul."

"Sweet dreams, love."

The screen went blank as Lord Mink terminated the call. Raoul had exactly one second to realize everyone had heard his last words to Iason.

"Sweet dreams, love," Xian immediately mocked in a teasing, high-pitched voice.

The other Blondies all snickered at this, except Raoul and Lord Sung, who both looked grumpy, and Megala Chi, who was holding his throat, still trying to recover from having nearly been strangled by Raoul.

At that moment Sir Elusiax Kain, who had been in the play room with Aki and Suuki for the entirety of the night, came into the great hall with both boys in tow, having no idea of the events that had taken place the night before.

He had heard a lot of laughing, shouting, and some strange sounds that he could not identify, and then had been somewhat surprised when—he assumed—the Blondies had apparently all gone to bed, for the whole house became strangely quiet. Now he entered the room, noting the broken chair that still lay on the floor against one wall, and looked around fearfully, afraid of what else he might see.

"Where's Iason?" he asked.

"Good morning, Sir Elusiax," Omaki said. "I'm afraid Iason had to go home. He had a headache."

"Oh, I see. Well, I'll just take Aki home with me, then," the Elite decided.

"That's an excellent idea. Iason may not be feeling well today," Lord Ghan replied. "We're all a bit hung over, as you may guess."

"I see. Well, then, I'll just be on my way."

"Won't you have some breakfast first?" Omaki offered, wondering if, in fact, there *was* any breakfast forthcoming. He wasn't entirely sure what attendants were still in his house and what they were up to.

"No, no, I'll have breakfast at home. I hope you had a good time. Your party sounded very…interesting." The Elite offered an artificially frozen smile, which was actually more than Lord Ghan expected.

"Oh, thank you! I believe it was quite a success. There were a few…issues…but everything got resolved in the end," Omaki said happily. "You should have come upstairs and joined us."

"Oh, no," Sir Elusiax said quickly, and then, catching himself, continued, "that is, I was quite comfortable where I was for the night. I wouldn't think of intruding on your special company."

"Oh, they're not special," Lord Ghan exclaimed. "You could have joined us."

"Gee thanks, Omaki," Xian snorted.

"Yes, Omaki, now that we know your true sentiments, perhaps it's time this party broke up," Heiku said, rising.

"Oh, don't go," Lord Ghan pleaded. "Stay another night. Last night hardly counted!"

"I'm afraid I've got to get back to the University," Lord Sung said, rising as well.

Aertis, taking his cue, stood up.

"I didn't mean to break up the party," Sir Elusiax said, frowning.

"Well, I'm going," Raoul announced.

Megala stood up and tried to speak, but found he couldn't.

"Megala, I'm going to the hospital; why don't you come with me," Lord Quiahtenon suggested. "We'll have your throat checked out."

Lord Chi nodded, looking fearfully at Raoul, who was still glaring at him.

"Everyone's leaving," Omaki said sadly. "You all had a terrible time. You're even leaving without breakfast."

The Blondies all groaned at this, reassuring Lord Ghan that they did, in fact, have a good time at his party—at least up until they were attacked by Federation rebels and had to go on a rescue mission in an Alphazenian vessel no one but Yousi knew how to fly.

"Coffee was enough for me," Heiku proclaimed, looking at Yousi. "I'm good to go."

Yousi was the last to stand up. "It was a very nice party," he said politely.

"Thank you, Yousi," Omaki said glumly.

Once the Blondies made their intention to leave clear, their pets and attendants appeared as if out of nowhere, except for those who were still at the hospital.

"The next party will be at my new seaside resort," Lord Am announced, looking pointedly at Megala Chi, "which I can assume will be built very quickly? Not in one year, like you stated before?"

Megala nodded furiously, tried to speak, and then put his hands to his throat.

"Very good. Why don't we set a date. Let's say two weeks from now? Can you manage that?"

Lord Chi seemed to think about this for a moment, calculating uncertainly, and then, realizing that Raoul wouldn't accept anything but a 'yes' for an answer, finally nodded.

"Hooray, another party," Yousi said gleefully.

The Blondies all cheered, lifting their half-empty coffee mugs as if to toast the date.

"It will be hard to top one of Omaki's parties, Raoul," Lord Sami warned.

Lord Ghan perked up at this. "Why, thank you, Xian," he said with a bow.

"You think I can't throw a good party?" Lord Am demanded.

"I don't think you've ever done it before, is all."

"Well, you just wait and see. It will be the best party you've all ever been to." His gaze moved to Sir Elusiax, who was inching toward the door. "And you're invited too, Elusiax, if you want to come and see my new seaside resort."

"Me? Well, I'll have to check my…social calendar. But thank you for the invitation."

"I don't know how you can sit around planning more parties when none of you have the Code memorized yet," Lord Sung complained.

The Blondies all groaned.

"We're not sitting," Yousi pointed out. "All of us are standing."

Heiku tried not to snort at this, fearing a warning look from the Headmaster. "Yes, and it's time to go," he said. "Thank you, Omaki, for a delightful party, one that will not be easily forgotten."

Ima was at his side, although Sarius was still at the hospital.

Omaki bowed. "It was my pleasure."

Xian put a hand on Lord Ghan's shoulder. "Send me a copy of those tapes," he whispered, winking.

"Will do," Omaki promised. They both bit their lips to keep from laughing as Headmaster Sung and Aertis made their way out the door, bidding farewell.

"I want a copy, too," Raoul said, overhearing.

"And I," Heiku agreed.

Megala waved his hand, trying to get Omaki's attention.

"Don't worry, you'll all get copies," Lord Ghan assured them.

IASON TERMINATED THE CALL, NOTICING that the Blondie had called him, perhaps accidentally, by an old affectionate term of endearment—*love*. For a brief moment he remembered what it had been like to be in Raoul's arms. Then he remembered Anori.

He sighed, turning away from the terminal.

Riki was leaning against a wall, watching him, a cigarette in his mouth.

"Riki, you know you can't smoke in here," Iason said in a scolding tone.

"It's not lit."

"Well, I'm just telling you."

"Even after all we've been through?"

"I don't want my penthouse to smell like smoke," the Blondie answered. "Let's not argue."

"Sheesh. Whatever. It's just a dumb old cigarette. I'll go out to the balcony, then."

"I'll go with you."

"Iason?"

"Yes?"

Riki took the cigarette from his mouth so he could open the sliding door to the balcony. "You and Raoul were lovers once, isn't that right?"

"Yes, Riki. You know that."

"He still has the hots for you."

Lord Mink was silent for a moment. "I know," he conceded, finally.

"You really don't have feelings for him?" Riki pressed.

"Raoul is…a good friend. That's all."

"But you loved him once?"

"Yes," Iason admitted.

"Then what happened?"

"I've told you this story before, haven't I?"

Riki lit up his cigarette, sitting up on the balcony ledge. "Tell me again."

Lord Mink sighed. "It was a long time ago. We were lovers at the Academy. Then Anori Khosi came from Alpha Zen. He was a handsome young dignitary, and Raoul fell for him. And…well, I told you the rest of the story."

"Anori Khosi—Voshka's brother, you mean?"

"Precisely."

"So what happened, exactly? Raoul cheated on you?"

"Yes, he did. And I caught him, and it was never the same after that."

"What happened to Anori?"

"Riki, I know I've told you this."

"Have you? I don't remember."

"I'm surprised you'd forget something like that."

"Oh! I remember now. You were jealous."

"More than just that. Come now, you haven't really forgotten, have you?"

"No," Riki admitted. "You were so jealous that you killed Anori. Isn't that right?"

Lord Mink bowed his head, closing his eyes. "Yes, I did," he answered.

Riki was silent for a moment. "So what was Vosh so upset about?" he asked, finally.

"After Anori died, we hid his vessel at Minas Qentu. No one knew about it except Raoul and Jupiter. We told the Commander that Anori had died in a crash. But apparently, when you and I were held hostage, Raoul and the others with him activated that ship to come and rescuc us."

"Really? They were going to rescue us?"

"Yes, they went after us and actually captured Amon Qentu, in fact, but by activating the ship, they triggered an alarm on Alpha Zen that identified the vessel as the ship belonging to Anori."

"Woah. So Vosh knows he was lied to."

"Yes, and he wasn't happy about it."

"What did you tell him?"

"I told him about the assassination. I just didn't tell him who did it."

"No, you can't do that," Riki asserted. "He'd kill you, for sure. So they really captured Amon Qentu? That fuck. What are they going to do with him?"

"Raoul says he was given to Yutaku Iman as a pet," Iason reported.

"Who the hell is Yutaku Iman?"

"He is a respected Blondie who lives in the villa next to Omaki. Apparently he went with them on the rescue mission."

"Well, I hope he beats the shit out of him after what he did to us!"

"I doubt that he will," Iason answered. "I think this was Konami's idea to force Yutaku into being a proper Master to a pet. He currently doesn't have a pet, you see, and he has all sorts of wild notions about it being wrong to have pets at all."

"Hmmmm. I think I like this Yutaku Iman, after all," Riki said, grinning.

"Riki," Iason sighed, rolling his eyes.

YUTAKU STOOD BY THE DOOR, STARING at the motionless figure who was manacled to the bed. He couldn't believe that it was really the infamous Amon Qentu who was in his hands, or that Konami Sung truly expected him to transform the notorious rebel into a pet.

He was, in truth, terrified. How could he possibly tame the great lord into submission?

Amon groaned, his eyes flickering open.

Lord Iman stepped forward. "Ah. You're coming to."

The man blinked a few times, finally focusing on Yutaku. "Who the hell are you?"

"I am…your new Master, actually. I mean, definitely. I'm Yutaku Iman. And I know who *you* are, of course."

Amon seemed to realize at that point that he was restrained. He struggled against his manacles, grimacing. "Release me!"

"I'm afraid I can't do that. Not until you're more… more… um… *compliant*, shall we say."

"What are you talking about?" Amon demanded.

"Perhaps I wasn't clear. You see, you were captured at the, uh, your mansion, and Lord Sung gave you to me to tame as a pet."

"Who the fuck is Lord Sung?"

"Pet, please don't say, 'fuck'. It's vulgar. I don't like vulgar language. Konami Sung is Head of the Eos Disciplinary Committee. He's been on me forever about not having a pet, you see, and—well, that's beside the point. The point is, you are now my pet. I know this must come as a shock to you, and I'm sorry for it, but the sooner you accept your situation, the better it will be for you."

"You can't just leave me chained up like this," Amon answered.

"I don't intend to, but it seemed necessary, at least at first."

"I need to take a piss."

Lord Iman trembled at this, having completely overlooked such a vulgar, though natural, bodily consideration.

"Then, I suppose I could release you and accompany you to the facilities."

Amon stared back at him unblinkingly, saying nothing.

"Now, don't give me any trouble," Yutaku warned, trying to sound as stern as possible. "Or I shall have to…punish you."

He pushed a button on the wall panel that released Amon from his manacles. The moment the man was free, he leapt to his feet and charged at Yutaku.

Amon was a strong man. But he was no match for a Blondie's strength.

Lord Iman, though surprised at the attack, quickly and easily subdued Amon, pulling his arms behind him and forcing him down to his knees. "Now pet," he scolded, "what did I just tell you? That was very naughty."

"Ow! You're hurting me!"

"Stop resisting me!"

Amon, realizing that he was in danger of having one of his arms pulled out of its socket, immediately relaxed, allowing Lord Iman to pull him to his feet.

"Did you really have to use the facilities?" Yutaku asked.

"Not really," Amon admitted.

"Well, then, get back on the bed. You'll have to be restrained again."

Surprisingly, Amon complied, the man having decided that he had horribly underestimated the Blondie's strength. Once he was restrained again, Lord Iman started to leave the room, turning at the door. "I shall contemplate your punishment now. I will return when I have made my decision." With that, he parted, leaving Amon to stare after him.

KONAMI SUNG DECIDED HE COULDN'T RISK calling Xanthus Kahn—not with Jupiter or her Sentinels overhearing. And he didn't own an Independent Channel device. So he was forced to pay the Blondie a personal visit to his private seaside estate, something he rarely did. He made the call the day Iason had returned to the penthouse, the first thing in the morning, as soon as he left Omaki's villa.

Lord Kahn's attendant answered the door and announced him; Xanthus looked more than surprised to see him.

"What brings you here so early, Headmaster?" he asked.

"The truth is, I've come on a rather delicate matter," Lord Sung admitted.

"I see," Lord Kahn said, crossing his arms on his chest.

"It involves myself and a…a student, actually. We both need to be disciplined, but we need the matter to be kept discrete, if at all possible."

Xanthus regarded him for a long moment. "You, Konami?"

Lord Sung bowed his head, ashamed. "Yes. I'm afraid so."

"You're telling me you engaged in relations with a student and you want both of you to be disciplined, but you want me to keep quiet about it?"

"Yes, precisely. If you don't mind."

"Well, I'll be honest with you. You're putting me in a position, here. If Jupiter were to find out, I would be punished for it."

"I realize that. If it's too much to ask, I understand. I shouldn't have come here and wasted your time."

Xanthas raised a hand to stay him. "Hold on. I didn't say I wouldn't do it. I just need a moment to think about it."

"Take as long as you like. You can call me with your answer—a simple yes or no, and the day we should come, if yes."

"You want to come together?"

"If that's possible?"

"I don't know if that's wise," Lord Kahn said.

"I promised Aertis," Konami explained.

"Aertis? Aertis Jin? You mean you seduced the brightest young Blondie at the Academy?" Xanthus demanded.

"I know it's unconscionable," Lord Sung agreed.

"It certainly is. And *if* I agree to punish you, you *will* be severely punished. Both of you."

Konami nodded. He had expected no less from Lord Kahn. "Very well. I'll leave you, then. Just let me know your decision."

"I will," Xanthus promised.

Konami left him then, finding that he was actually trembling. He caught himself and smiled. After all, Xanthus was a former student. But the Blondie was a formidable disciplinarian, that much was true enough. And if he did agree to punish the two of them, it wouldn't be pleasant.

HEIKU QUIAHTENON WAS JUST ABOUT to have his breakfast when an incoming call came in from the Academy.

"Ah. They've found the father," he proclaimed, snapping open his handheld. "Heiku Quiahtenon here."

"Sir? This is the Lead Technician over at the Laboratory. We're doing the testing on your…pet, Ima, and, as you know, we've not found any matches with any Academy-bred pets, according to our database."

"Yes, yes," Lord Quiahtenon said impatiently. "I know this already."

"Well, what we have discovered is…uh…a possible match with, that is, with someone who has mongrel blood."

Heiku stood very still. "And how would you know that?"

"We did some random testing of mongrels to be sure."

"And what are you suggesting?"

"Well, we know of a certain pet who is not registered with the Academy, so we can't pull up his profile, but this said pet has mongrel blood."

"You mean Iason's pet, Riki."

"Precisely."

"I'll kill him. If he touched my girl, I will kill him."

"Oh, we don't know if it's him, for sure. We need his profile. We were wondering if you could approach Lord Mink about it?"

"You want *me* to bring it up with Iason?" Heiku laughed. "He'll be as angry as I am."

"Well," the man said, "that's why we were hoping you could sort of smooth things over with him. We don't think he'd give us the profile. But maybe if *you* talked to him?"

"Oh, I'll talk to him all right. I'll give him a piece of my mind. If Riki did this, I'll be furious. I don't want some half-mongrel bug."

"Yes, Sir. Of course not, Sir."

"If that's the case, we'll have to get rid of it."

"Ah, that may not be possible. She's pretty far along."

"What do you mean it's not possible? Are you saying she has to carry that mongrel's bastard to term?"

"Remember, we don't know for sure that it's Riki's child or not."

"Well, it's *some* mongrel's child! And who else could it be but Riki?"

"I don't know, Sir."

Lord Quiahtenon sighed. "Very well. I'll talk to Iason."

"Thank you, Sir."

Heiku ended the call, brooding for a few minutes. "Ima!" he bellowed.

Ima hurried into the hall, wearing a skimpy outfit, per usual, one that revealed a slight bulge in her tummy.

"Yes, Master?" she purred.

"I'm going to ask you this once. You had better answer me straight, Ima. I will know if you're lying. Do you understand me?"

"Yes," she answered, frowning.

"Did you sleep with Riki, Iason's pet?"

Ima blinked, looking so startled and guilty that Heiku knew, in that instant, that the mongrel had been with his girl.

"Did you, Ima?" he shouted.

Ima shook her head. "No, Master. Of course not."

"You're lying. I can tell."

"I'm…I'm not lying," she protested, eyes wide.

"Well, we're getting Riki's genetic profile, so we'll find out for sure. If I find out you're lying, you're getting the spanking of your life."

At this, Ima broke down, sobbing and pleading with her Master for mercy.

"I knew it," he hissed. "You naughty girl! Come here!"

Ima approached him slowly, begging not to be spanked.

"Oh, you're getting a spanking," Heiku said, grabbing her wrist and leading her over to a chair. He pulled her over his knee and lifted her miniskirt, tugging down her panties to her knees.

"It was only once!" Ima cried. "Please, Master!"

"When did it happen?"

"When Riki was in Midas. Honest, it was just the one time!"

"It makes no difference to me whether it was one time or a thousand. You're getting spanked, Ima."

"Please, Master!"

"Sarius!" Heiku bellowed.

Sarius, who had been watching this whole confrontation from the shadows, immediately appeared. "Yes, Master?"

"Bring me a paddle."

"Right away, Master."

"No, Master, nooooo!" Ima begged.

"You should have known better than to sleep with another pet—especially Iason's pet! Now you'll get what's coming to you! A sound paddling!"

Sarius rushed back into the room with the paddle, smiling slightly at Ima's predicament.

"Sarius, I want you to watch this. Let this be a lesson to *you,* that if I hear anything from this household on The Channel, you will be over my knees next."

Sarius blanched a little at this, nodding. "Yes, Master."

With that, Heiku began paddling Ima as hard as he could. The girl screamed and kicked, but the Blondie held her down over his knees, swatting her with the paddle until her cheeks were red as Aristian Red Emperor.

Afterwards she was sent to her room, and Heiku, still angry, placed an outgoing call on Independent to Iason Mink.

"Iason Mink," came the reply, low and sultry.

"Iason, I'll have you know I just paddled my Ima raw, and do you know why?"

A pause. "I'm sure I don't."

"Because she just admitted to me that she slept with Riki when he was in Midas. In fact, the Academy suspects that Riki is the father of her child."

Now there was a *long* pause on the line. Then, "Are you quite sure?"

"I'm sure they slept together. Whether or not Riki is the father, I don't know, but I don't see who else it could be. They specifically said it matched a mongrel blood-type. We need Riki's identification profile for a genetic match. Can you send it to the Academy?"

"Will do," Iason said. "Is that all?"

"Well, don't you want to talk about this? What do you mean, 'Is that all'?"

"Excuse me, I only meant…that I'm quite anxious to…confront Riki about this," Lord Mink explained.

"Ah. I see. Yes, of course," Heiku replied. "We can talk later."

"Very good." Iason disconnected the call, leaving Heiku holding the phone.

"Anyway, the mongrel's in for it," Lord Quiahtenon said, seeming somewhat consoled by the thought.

"OH SHU," VOSHKA SAID, IN BETWEEN kisses. "You don't know how long I've waited for this."

"Then, do you forgive me for running away?"

The Commander smiled. "I forgive you, but I'm still going to discipline you."

"What! But you just paddled me raw in front of the entire harem!"

"Ten years is a long time, my pet," Voshka said, kissing him again.

"Yes, you said that," Aranshu replied, breaking away. "But, Master—*Komiat*—doesn't my submission now count for something?"

"Oh, yes. I'm quite pleased."

"Then?"

"Perhaps I won't have to resort to corporal punishment, now that you're being so obedient," the man replied. "But make no mistake, Velo is part of your punishment."

Aranshu pouted at this. "That's not fair."

"Aranshu," Voshka said in a warning tone.

"You know how much I hate it!"

"Yes, I do. But you can hardly expect me to overlook ten years of defiance without some sort of reprimand?"

"But you don't understand," Aranshu wailed, tears in his eyes. "He was my only friend in the harem. Now, to find out he swooped in and took my place! It's infuriating!"

The Commander laughed softly. "He hardly swooped in, as you put it. I commanded him to my bed."

"But why him?"

"Because…I knew he was your friend. And he knew some Aristian. It made me feel…closer to you."

Aranshu thought about this for a moment. "But why did you keep him with you all these years as your pet?"

"Because he pleased me."

Frowning, Aranshu turned his head away.

Voshka took hold of his chin, forcing his attention. "Must I remind you that if you hadn't run away, I would have never invited Velo to my bed?"

"Do you like having sex with him more than me?"

At this, Voshka smiled. "Your jealousy is endearing."

"Well, do you? Is he better in bed than me?"

"Velo is very good in bed. I have trained him well."

"You didn't answer me. Do you prefer him to me?"

The Commander's eyes twinkled. "Perhaps you ought to think about that when we're in bed together, and do your very best."

Aranshu looked surprised. "But I thought you enjoyed our sex."

"Oh, I do. Don't misunderstand me. But there's always room for… improvement."

"You *do* prefer Velo!" Aranshu accused angrily.

"Shu," Voshka laughed.

"I could tell when you were loving him before! He pleases you!"

"Velo has been my pet for ten years," Voshka answered. "Of course he pleases me. Might I remind you that you voluntarily left that position vacant when you disappeared."

"But I thought…." Aranshu looked away.

The Commander gently took hold of his chin again, turning his head. "Yes? What is it you thought?"

"I thought we had something special," Aranshu said finally, his eyes glimmering with tears.

"Oh, Shu. We *do* have something special. Why do you think I searched the entire Quadrant for you? I was devastated when you left. You hurt me terribly."

"I'm sorry I hurt you. I was angry."

"I know you were. But you could have come back sooner."

"I had a hard time just surviving," Aranshu admitted. "After I ran out of funds, I mean. And I wanted to come back, but I was afraid of what you would do to me."

"But ten years?"

"I know. But…I thought about you…every single day."

The Commander sighed. "And I thought about you, Aranshu. I never stopped hoping I would find you. I admit I was angry—

extremely angry. I can see why you were afraid to come back. But surely you can see why I need companionship…and more."

"Did you utilize the harem, too?" Aranshu asked jealously.

Voshka laughed. "Of course I did."

"You've probably fucked hundreds of boys…and a few of them have fucked you!"

"Shu…."

"You know something? I never had sex with anyone else the whole time I was away. I could have. But I didn't."

The Commander studied him. "Is that true?"

"Yes, it's true."

"And why is that?"

"Because…I don't know, it's complicated."

"Because? Try to explain."

"Because my heart was tangled up with you," Aranshu answered finally.

Voshka smiled, his eyes shining with love. "Come here," he said, opening his arms.

Aranshu snuggled in his Master's arms, sighing. He felt safe in the man's embrace. This was where he wanted to be. He knew that now. Much as he hated to admit it, he knew it was true.

The Commander pushed him onto his back. He looked down at him, his eyes glimmering with desire.

"My heart…has always been tangled up with you, my sweet Shu," he whispered.

Aranshu said nothing. He felt like challenging this assertion with the fact that the Commander had enjoyed sex with so many others, including Velo, but he didn't want to ruin the moment.

"Kiss me," he said.

Voshka's lips met his in a passionate, consuming kiss. It was as if they couldn't get enough of each other. Aranshu put his hands in the Commander's hair, marveling at its softness.

Voshka's fingers were over his special gland, expertly stimulating him. He gasped, arching up against the Commander's body.

"You're quite ready for me," Voshka noted.

"Yes," Aranshu agreed.

"What do you want, my pet?"

"Straddle me," Aranshu begged.

Smiling at this, Voshka repositioned himself, straddling him, and slowly slid down on Aranshu's cock, accepting its entire length.

"Holy fuck," Aranshu gasped. "Oh, *Komiat!*"

The Commander rocked against him, all the while stroking the Aristian's special gland with one hand and holding his cock with the other.

Aranshu was wild with pleasure, arching his back and squealing.

Voshka laughed softly. "You like this, do you?"

"Yes! Gods yes!"

The Commander closed his eyes, letting his head fall back. "Mmmm. I think I've found my spot." He began thrusting and rocking in a particular way, grunting with each thrust.

Aranshu could take it no more. Voshka began to pump him with uncompromising strokes, determined to elicit the seed which soon came gushing out of his cock, spilling down his hand.

The Aristian cried out as though he were in agony, but Voshka knew otherwise. He smiled, watching his pet's glory.

Then he shifted positions and quickly reached his own ascent, welcoming the waves of pleasure that shot through his body.

It was sex, and Voshka had experienced plenty of sex in his years as Commander, and even before. But nothing compared to sex with Aranshu. Though he didn't want his pet to know it, Voshka was never truly satisfied unless he was with his Shu.

Despite ten years of countless young men in his bed, in addition to Velo, Voshka could never replicate the intoxicating experience of bedding his favorite pet.

And now, finally, he had him in his bed again. Everything would have been perfect, if there had not been something else weighing on his mind.

He was thinking of his brother's ship, and how upset Raoul had been when he called Iason Mink. A thought was pressing into his mind, a disturbing thought. A thought that had to do with Raoul and Iason.

And ultimately, with his brother.

LORD MINK SAT FOR A LONG TIME at his computer terminal after receiving Heiku's call. He sent Riki's identification profile to the Academy, frowning. Then he turned and saw Riki sitting out on the balcony ledge, smoking a cigarette.

Sighing, he got up and made his way out to the balcony.

"Pet, how many times must I tell you not to sit up on the balcony ledge? Do you want to fall to your death? Get down at once!"

"Sheesh, I'm not going to fall," Riki answered, though he did jump down from the ledge.

"Sometimes I think you do things deliberately to annoy me," Iason accused.

"I wasn't trying to annoy you. I just forgot. Anyway, I'm down." Riki stared at him, frowning. "What's wrong? Why are you pulling such a look?"

"I just got off the phone with Heiku Quiahtenon," Iason said.

"Oh, shit," Riki said.

"Riki," Iason sighed. "Don't tell me it's true?"

"That's the real reason I ran away. I didn't want you to find out about it," the mongrel admitted.

"You really had sexual relations with Ima?"

"Yeah."

"But why, Riki?"

"What do you mean, why? Have you seen her? She's hot as fuck!"

"Riki!"

"Well, I'm just a mongrel, remember? I have needs! And it was the week you let me go free in Midas."

"Be that as it may, I don't remember giving you permission to have sex with another pet," Iason said.

"Is that all you're mad about?"

"What do you mean, 'Is that all'? I'll have you know Heiku is furious about it. It appears you may be the father."

"She told me it might be someone else," Riki protested.

"And you believed her? As for that, we'll find out soon enough. I've had your identification profile sent to the Academy. They'll be able to tell whether it's a match."

Riki was silent for a moment. "I'm really sorry, Iason," he said finally.

Lord Mink made no answer. Then, "So you…enjoyed being intimate with her, I suppose?"

The mongrel smiled, tossing his cigarette over the ledge. "You don't have to be jealous."

"Riki, I've told you a thousand times to put your cigarette out in one of the ashtrays rather than throw it over the ledge! What if you catch someone's hair on fire?"

Riki frowned. "Oh. Sorry."

"You deliberately provoke me."

"I wasn't trying to provoke you, honest."

"She's the pet from the magazine," Iason stated, remembering.

"She means nothing to me. Honest." Riki said, his eyes shining. "She wasn't even that good of a fuck."

"I suppose you're saying that out of some sense of obligation to me."

"No. I'm serious. It wasn't mind-blowing sex, like we have. It was your average sex. Good, but average. She wasn't even that tight. Not like *you*. I didn't fuck her up the ass, you know."

Iason seemed to relax a little, shaking his head. "Riki, what am I going to do with you? Can you stay out of trouble for even one day?"

"What, you're not going to punish me, are you?"

The Blondie laughed. "Did you think I would let that go without some kind of punishment?"

"After what we just went through?"

Master and pet gazed at each other for a long moment.

"I don't want to punish you, Riki. But my hands are tied," Iason said softly.

"What do you mean?"

"I mean, unsanctioned pet pairing requires mandatory punishment as laid down in the Code. It's not that severe—just a paddling, I believe."

"What! You're going to paddle me?" Riki demanded.

"Riki," Iason sighed. "What did you expect I would do?"

"I don't know, but I think a paddling fucking sucks—especially after we just went through the most horrific day possible together."

"I know, pet," Lord Mink whispered. "I'm sorry, there's nothing I can do about it. Heiku will be calling back, demanding to know how I handled it with you."

"I'd rather *he* do it than you do it," Riki said glumly.

Iason was quiet for a moment. "Are you sure about that? He sounded quite angry."

"I'm sick of you punishing me," Riki said. "It makes me angry at you. Please, just have him do it."

"Very well. I'll arrange it."

At that moment, Yui arrived, entering the penthouse with the special passcode that had been given him.

"Ah," Iason said. "It appears we have an attendant."

"Yui?" Riki asked, looking through the double doors that led to the balcony into the great hall.

"Yes, Raoul is lending him to us for a spell, until Toma returns from the hospital."

"Good, because I'm hungry."

"Then I'll have him prepare us some food."

"Iason?"

"Yes?"

"If the baby is mine, could we keep it?"

Lord Mink didn't answer right away. "Let me think on it, Riki," he said finally.

HEADMASTER SUNG WAS SITTING BY THE FIRE when his phone began to chime with an incoming call from Xanthus Kahn. He answered the call, trying not to seem nervous.

"Yes? Have you an answer for me?"

"I do. I've decided I'll do it."

"Excellent. Thank you, Xanthus."

"Come by tomorrow at the seventh hour, in the evening," Lord Kahn continued.

"Seven," Sung repeated. "Very good."

"I'll see you then." Xanthus disconnected the call without another word.

Konami let the phone fall into his lap, trembling.

YUTAKU SAT IN HIS CHAIR BY THE WINDOW, LOOKING out at Lake Erphanes. He had no idea what he was going to do with Amon, or how he was going to punish him. In fact, just the thought of punishing such a man made him feel queasy. A great leader like Amon Qentu, coming from a long line of ancient kings? It wasn't right, and he felt angry with Headmaster Sung for forcing him to take Amon as a pet.

He finally decided that he would *not* punish the man. *This* time. After all, what would he do if he were in Amon's place? Surely he would resist being manacled, too.

The man was probably hungry. He called his attendant, Orin, and asked him to have a tray of food brought.

"If it's not too much trouble," he added.

"No, Master, of course it's not any trouble," Orin said, bowing. He was accustomed to his Master's ways, and found it endearing that the man was always so polite when requesting something. No other Master on Amoi was like that.

Yutaku rose, sighing. He would have to talk to Amon. The man probably *did* need to use the facilities, now.

He went into the room where Amon was shackled. The man glared at him.

"I hate seeing a great man such as you manacled in such a way," Yutaku began.

Amon seemed surprised at this remark, softening his gaze, though he said nothing.

"It wasn't my idea for you to be my pet," Yutaku continued. "I'm opposed to the whole notion of Masters and pets, you see. I'm something of a deviant, I guess you could say. But Lord Sung—he's Head of the Eos Disciplinary Committee—he insisted that I take you as a pet. You see, I haven't had a pet in years. And he noticed that I…took an interest in you."

At this Amon frowned, seeming puzzled.

"You look like you have something to say," Yutaku encouraged.

"How do you know me?" Amon asked.

"Oh," Yutaku said, taking a few steps closer, "everyone's heard of you. Goodness! You're a legend! A great man such as you? It pains me to see you humbled in such a way. I would release you— if I could trust you."

"And my punishment?"

"I've decided you're not to be punished. I would have done the same thing if I were in your position, I think. But try it again, and I *will* have to punish you."

Amon seemed to think about this for a moment. "You're not like the others," he said softly.

"No, I'm not," Lord Iman agreed.

"You're strong, though. It's true what they say about Blondies—you have incredible strength."

"You're strong, too," Yutaku said, though he was flattered at the compliment. "You must take good care of your body."

"That I do."

"As a physician, I can't help but note what incredible shape you're in. Marvelous."

Amon almost smiled, regarding Yutaku with a friendlier look. "You'll take these manacles off?"

"Can I trust you?"

"Yes. They're most uncomfortable. And this time, I really *do* need to relieve myself."

"I thought as much. All right."

Yutaku cautiously released the man of his manacles, gripping him firmly as he did so.

"Why don't you want a pet?" Amon asked.

"Because…well it's simply unconscionable in my view, the whole system. Why should anyone submit to a Master?"

"I quite agree with you," Amon said glumly.

"Yes, I'm quite sorry about all this. As I said—it wasn't my idea. But if you could just trust me, I assure you I'll give you nearly all the liberties you could want."

"What about my freedom?"

"Except that," Yutaku answered. "I'm sorry. And I must warn you: if you try to escape, there is severe punishment awaiting you. It's outlined in the Code and my hands are tied, there."

Amon nodded. "The facilities?"

"Come, I'll take you." Yutaku led Amon through the villa, keeping one hand firmly on his shoulder. But surprisingly, this time, Amon did not try to resist.

When they got to the bath hall, Amon hesitated. "I don't suppose I could have some privacy?"

Yutaku nodded. "Of course. I'll be waiting outside. Take a bath, if you want, or a shower."

"I could use one," Amon admitted. "You're not going to insist on bathing me?"

"Oh, no," Yutaku assured him. "I wouldn't dream of intruding on your privacy. When you're finished, there's food waiting for you."

Amon gave him a slight nod, disappearing into the bath hall.

Yutaku let out a great sigh of relief. He felt his interactions with Amon were proceeding quite well; the man wasn't even resisting him now. He waited and smiled when he heard the water to the bath. So. The man had chosen to bathe. This thought reminded him that he had no wardrobe for his pet; frowning, he put out an urgent outgoing call on Independent to the tailor in Eos, asking if he could come to his villa.

"What size is your pet?" the tailor asked.

"Well he's…quite large. Almost as tall as me."

"What?" the tailor seemed confused.

"It's Amon Qentu," Yutaku explained.

"You mean the notorious Federation rebel?"

"Precisely."

"Goodness. That will cost you extra, due to his size. It will require more fabric and—"

"That's no problem. Do you have anything you can bring right away?"

"The only thing that would fit him are Blondie clothes," the tailor answered.

"Fine. Bring something."

"But, are you sure?"

"Yes, yes, I'm sure," Yutaku snapped, irritated.

"Very well. I'll be there within the hour."

"Thank you."

Yutaku cut the transmission, still standing outside the bath hall.

"Amon," he called gently.

"Yes?"

"About your clothes…I'm afraid you'll have to wear the outfit you came in, for now, when you finish with your bath. I'll have something new for you to put on within the hour, however."

There was a slight pause. "Whatever."

"Very good. How is the bath?"

"Nice," Amon conceded. "You have quite a setup, here."

"And the tub accommodates you?"

"Yes, I have plenty of room."

"Good. Let me know if you need anything. You should find shampoo and other items on the shelf, there, by the tub."

"I see it."

"Then, I'll leave you to your bath."

Amon made no reply, and Yutaku smiled, wondering what the man looked like, lying naked in his tub. He immediately regretted the thought, cursing himself. It wasn't right to debase Amon by thinking of him in such a way, he thought.

But then, Amon *was* his pet. Headmaster Sung would expect Amon to perform for him. But how would he convince the proud Federation rebel to do something like that?

RIKI FOLLOWED IASON INSIDE THE PENTHOUSE, silently watching when the Blondie made for the bar and poured himself a brandy.

Yui came running from the kitchen. "I'm sorry, Lord Mink. I could have gotten that for you."

"I know my way around the bar," Iason replied.

"Dinner will be ready as soon as possible," Yui said.

"Excellent."

Yui rushed back into the kitchen.

Riki frowned. "Are you mad at me?"

"No," Lord Mink answered.

"No?"

Iason sighed, making his way to his chair. "Perhaps a little."

"I thought so. You only drink brandy when you're mad. Like I said, she means nothing to me."

"I'm glad to hear it."

"For the record, I seem to remember that you paired with cat-boy when I was gone," Riki said.

Lord Mink sat down in his chair and took a drink of brandy. "Riki, I'm the Master of this house."

"Yeah, I know. You're the Master, and I'm just the stupid fucking pet."

"Riki."

"What? It's so unfair. You can do whatever *you* want, but I can't do anything. I should be able to punish you for sleeping with cat-boy."

"We're not going to have this discussion. Come here."

Riki sauntered over to his Master's chair, hands in his pockets.

"Sit down, on my lap."

Riki did so, snuggling up to the Blondie. He played with Iason's hair, wrapping it around his fingers. "I love you, Iason."

Lord Mink softened at this, smiling. "Do you, Riki?"

"Yeah. I just told you, didn't I?"

"If you love me, why did you sleep with Ima?"

"Oh, come on. Why did you sleep with cat-boy?"

"Answer me."

Riki sighed. "I don't even know why, honestly. She's been a fantasy of mine since…forever." He hesitated when he saw the Blondie's frown. "I mean, she *is* hot. You've seen her body, right?"

"I've seen it," Iason said thoughtfully. "So, did you prefer being intimate with her?"

"Fuck no," Riki laughed. "You should know that."

"It was the same with me and Enyu," Lord Mink replied. "I suppose I enjoyed it, but only because you weren't around for me to be with. But the experience was…hollow. It left me unsatisfied."

"Yeah. That's it exactly. It's different when you really love someone."

"And you really love me, then?" Iason pressed.

At that moment, Iason's handheld chimed with an incoming message from Heiku Quiahtenon.

Iason gave Riki a warning look. "It's Heiku," he said.

"Oh, fuck," Riki groaned.

"Iason Mink," the Blondie answered.

"Iason. I assume you've had time to confront Riki about the encounter?" Heiku asked.

"Yes, I have. He's admitted to it as well."

"And what did you do to him?" Heiku asked, sounding a little angry.

"Nothing, yet. Riki asked that *you* administer the punishment."

Surprised, Heiku nearly dropped the phone. "He did, did he? Well, I can certainly do that. Why yes, I'd be more than happy to help out with that. When should I stop by?"

"Let's make it tomorrow."

"Tomorrow? But—"

"Riki and I have just been through an ordeal. He needs at least one more night to recover."

"Well, yes, I suppose that's true," Heiku conceded. "But tell him I'm bringing my paddle."

"Will do."

"But let me get to the reason I called: it's a match."

"What?" Iason asked, puzzled.

"The genetic profile you sent to the Academy. I mean Riki and Ima. It's a match."

Lord Mink was silent as the full weight of this sunk in. "What are you going to do about it?"

"That's the thing. They say she's too far along to get rid of the bug. But I don't want to deal with it!"

"We'll take the child," Iason said.

"What? Are you serious?"

"I'm serious. Riki wants it, and we'll find a way to take care of it."

"Well, I must say, I'm relieved. Although I hope you know what you're doing, Iason. A child? Don't you have enough on your hands?"

"I'm already the Guardian for Aki," Iason replied, "so it won't make much difference to be Guardian to another child."

Riki listened to this conversation in disbelief. Although he couldn't hear what Heiku said, he could tell from Iason's responses what was going on. He was going to be a father! And Iason was going to let him keep the child!

"If you're sure. What time tomorrow, then?" Heiku asked.

"Let's make it the second hour after noon."

"Very well. See you tomorrow, then."

"Good night, Heiku."

Iason disconnected the call, looking at Riki, who seemed overjoyed.

"It's really true, then? I'm going to be a father?"

"I'm not pleased with the idea of your being permanently attached to Ima in some way," Iason said, "but yes, you're going to be a father."

"And you're going to let me keep the child?"

"Yes, I am, Riki. We'll raise him, or her, together."

"I hope it's a boy," Riki said, leaning back against him. "This is going to be awesome! But wait—he won't be a pet, will he?"

"No," Iason answered. "I'll be his—or her—Guardian. The child will go to the Elite Academy, same as Aki."

"You'd do that for me? Why?"

"Because," Iason said, looking deep into his eyes, "I love you, Riki."

"You're gonna make me cry. Shit."

"Your punishment is tomorrow afternoon. Heiku is bringing a paddle."

"Well, fuck. That sucks."

"Riki," Iason admonished.

"But you can hardly expect me to be excited about getting paddled, can you? Especially by a Blondie with a robotic arm!"

"You're the one who wanted Heiku to do it," Lord Mink reminded him.

"I know. It's just...I feel like ever since I got here, I've been punished every day."

"You have this one coming, Riki. You knew better than to pair with a pet."

"I know, I know," Riki sighed.

"Then why did you do it?"

"I wish I knew."

"Then, if you had the chance again, you wouldn't?"

"No, I wouldn't," Riki said firmly. "Especially because I know how much it hurt you."

At this, the Blondie softened. "Yes, you did hurt me, Riki. But...I forgive you."

"Iason?"

"Yes?"

"Let's go make love."

"Oh, Riki," Lord Mink whispered. "I don't know if you've ever said that to me."

"Haven't I?"

Iason put down his drink on the table next to his chair, and stood up. Riki wrapped his legs around the Blondie, and Lord Mink carried him to the bedroom and laid him on the bed.

Iason moved on top of the mongrel, kissing him. "Riki, Riki," he breathed.

"I'm fucking turned on as hell," Riki whispered.

"Take off your shirt," Iason directed.

Riki did so, and the Blondie immediately began suckling one of his nipples.

"Oh yeah," Riki said, arching his back. "Right there!"

"Pet, you excite me beyond bearing."

The two of them then began kissing, rolling around on the bed together.

"Why don't you get undressed?" Riki suggested.

"You, as well," the Blondie answered, as he began taking off his tunic.

"One thing I love about you is your hair," the mongrel said, reaching out to touch a strand of Iason's beautiful white mane. "Yours is the best of all the Blondies."

"And I love your dark hair and eyes," Iason answered.

Riki shrugged. "I'm nothing special."

Iason took off his boots and then unzipped his bodysuit, shaking it off. Finally, he took off his gloves. "You're special to me. Get undressed, Riki."

The mongrel unzipped his pants, tauntingly pulling them down to his hips. He wore no underwear, per usual.

Lord Mink stood, completely naked, hands on his hips. "You're teasing me."

"Do you like it?"

"I want to see *all* of you. Strip. And lie back on the bed."

"Oh, all right." Riki tugged down his pants and then kicked them off, lying back on the bed as instructed. "You're so sexy, Iason."

"Am I?" The Blondie crawled toward him, a smoldering look in his eyes.

"Gods, yes," Riki answered, swallowing hard. "Shit! I'm so turned on I can barely think! I love it when you give me that look."

"What would you like, my pet?"

"Could you suck me?"

"Mmmm." Iason repositioned himself between the mongrel's legs.

"Oh, yeah," Riki breathed, when the Blondie began working him. "Your mouth is so hot…and wet…and oooo I love it when you flick your tongue along the head like that! Yeah! Just like that!"

Iason looked up at him as he serviced him, his eyes burning with lust.

"Sexy! You're so sexy, Iason! Fuck! That's perfect! Hey this time, why don't I come on your face? Can I?"

Lord Mink hesitated for a moment.

"What, you don't like that?"

"I thought we were going to make love," the Blondie said softly.

"That *is* making love. At least the way I do it," Riki protested. "Please?"

"Very well," Iason conceded, continuing to lap him up.

Riki put his hands on the Blondie's head. "I'm not going to last very long, this time. I don't know why, but I'm excited. *You* excite me. You look so sexy, my cock in your mouth and your hair everywhere, and ohhhh, oh my God, oh fuck, it's coming, I'm gonna come, don't move, here it is—"

With that, the mongrel came on his Master's face, groaning his pleasure. "Fuck yeah! Oh fuck yeah!"

When he was finished, Iason got up and retrieved a towel, wiping his face. Then he threw it aside, crawling onto the bed again.

"That was fucking amazing!" Riki announced, grinning. "My cum all over your face! You should have seen the look on your face just now! Holy shit!"

"Riki," Iason breathed, "turn over."

"Hmmm? Yeah, okay." The mongrel flipped onto his stomach, continuing to smile. "But I hope you were planning to use some oil."

Lord Mink reached for a vial of oil, knocking over a lamp, and pouring out the entire contents onto his cock.

"Do you think you put enough on?" Riki teased, looking over his shoulder.

"Oh, pet," Iason moaned, as his hand slid up and down his lubricated cock.

"How is it *you* can knock over a lamp and not get in trouble?"

"Riki, I am Master of this house," Iason said impatiently. "Spread your legs open wide for me."

"Go slow, okay? Master Blondie of the house?"

Lord Mink slowly penetrated him from behind, making a grunting sound.

The mongrel laughed.

"Riki," Iason scolded.

"You just sound like some wild animal, is all."

"Oh pet; you're gripping me exquisitely."

The mongrel closed his eyes. "You slid right in this time. All that oil made a difference."

Iason moved against him, groaning.

"Yeah, fuck me, Blondie," the mongrel hissed.

"Riki, Riki!"

"Oh! Right there! You're hitting my spot!"

"Here?" Iason thrust repeatedly in the same area, making the mongrel cry out each time.

"Oh fuck! You're gonna make me come again! You're fucking me so good!"

"I'm not fucking you, I'm making love to you," Lord Mink clarified.

"No, you're definitely *fucking* me. Holy shit!"

Then, for no apparent reason, Iason began speaking in another entirely different language. "*Havar fornis tuu, repitar o repitar, myri Eroni.*"

Riki laughed. "What the fuck? I don't know what language that is, but that's sexy as hell."

"It's Alphazenian."

"What did you say to me?"

"I said, 'I'm going to fuck you over and over, my pet.'"

"Cool! Hey! Maybe you should teach me Alphazenian in case we ever fuck Vosh again."

Iason frowned. "Riki." He reached out and gave the mongrel a hard slap on the buttocks.

"I was just kidding! Sheesh! You Blondies have no sense of humor."

"I have a sense of humor. But not in bed," Lord Mink replied.

"I'm gonna come in like, two seconds," Riki warned.

"Come for me, my love."

"Holy shit," the mongrel groaned.

"I'm on your heels," Iason said through clenched teeth. Then, with a spine-tingling cry, the Blondie spent his seed.

Iason lay on top of the mongrel for a few minutes, breathing hard.

"You're crushing me," the mongrel protested. "But that was awesome."

"Oh, Riki," Iason said, rolling off him and onto his side.

"Was it good for you?" Riki joked.

"Pet…that was magnificent. Riki?"

"Yeah?"

"Did you really mean what you said before? That you love me?"

"Yeah, I meant it. I love you, Iason."

"Riki," Lord Mink breathed. "I love you so much I can hardly bear it."

LATER, AT DINNER, IASON'S HANDHELD began to chime again. The Blondie frowned. "That's odd. It's Heiku again."

"He must really be mad," Riki said, getting up from the table. "I'm finished. I'm going to the gardens."

Lord Mink nodded, and then answered the phone. "Iason Mink."

"Iason, I'm sorry to disturb you again, but I thought you'd want to know this."

"Yes?"

"Ima just miscarried. I'm at the hospital now."

"I see," Iason said after a short pause.

"I really should have known better, as a physician. I did paddle her pretty hard. Perhaps, deep inside, I was hoping for something like this."

"What's done is done."

"I suppose that's true."

"Was it—?"

"It was a boy."

"Ah. Riki wanted a boy," Iason said thoughtfully.

"I'm sorry, I guess he won't be getting the child like we'd thought."

"It can't be helped now. I'll tell him."

"Then, I'll see you tomorrow."

"Until then."

The Blondie disconnected the phone, sitting for a moment at the table. He thought about how excited Riki had been about being a father and he dreaded having to tell him the news.

After a moment, he got up and went out to the gardens, where he found his pet sitting on a bench, looking happy.

"I love this garden," Riki said, smiling.

"I'm glad it pleases you," Iason answered, sitting down next to him.

"So what did Heiku want? To talk about my punishment?"

Iason shook his head. "No, love. There's something I have to tell you."

At this, Riki frowned. "Well, shit. I can tell by your look that it isn't good."

"I'm sorry, Riki. But Ima lost the baby."

The mongrel seemed shocked for a moment, saying nothing. Then, "Fuck." His voice broke as he reached up and wiped a tear from his face.

"Oh, Riki."

"That was, like, probably the only chance I'll ever have at being a father."

Lord Mink nodded, unsure of what to say to this. "I'm terribly sorry," he said, finally. "I know you wanted it."

"I did. I did want it."

"Come here." Iason held out his arms, and Riki buried his face against the Blondie's chest, weeping. They remained thus for several minutes, Master and pet, the mongrel grieving his loss.

"Iason?"

"Yes, love?"

"Was it a boy?"

Lord Mink nodded. "Yes."

"Shit. I would have named him Guy, you know. Just to honor the poor bloke's memory."

Privately, Iason was glad the child had been lost, if Riki had been planning to name him after his old lover. He wasn't sure if he would have been able to be kind to the child with the constant memory of Riki's pairing partner coming to mind every time he said the boy's name.

"We still have Aki," he said gently. "We can raise him together."

"That's true," Riki replied. "I hadn't really thought of that."

"Speaking of which, I can only assume Aki is with Sir Elusiax," Lord Mink said, suddenly standing. "I should go ferret out his whereabouts."

"I'll stay here for a few minutes."

"As you wish."

Iason went back inside, and was just crossing the great hall when an incoming beacon sounded on his home terminal.

From Voshka Khosi.

Frowning, he went over to his terminal and sat down, punching in the code to answer the call.

Voshka came onscreen, looking more intense than usual.

"Commander," Iason said, nodding slightly.

"Oh, I see. We're back to 'Commander', are we?"

"What can I do for you, Vosh?"

The man's lip quivered slightly. "That's better. I have a few matters to discuss with you, actually. The first is regarding my pet, Aranshu."

Iason frowned, puzzled. "Yes?"

"I'm convinced he's part Blondie, and I'd like to determine who the father is," the Commander said.

Lord Mink smiled. "You must be mistaken. Blondies are sterile."

"So they say. However, I've fucked a Blondie or two in my day, and I know what it feels like. Aranshu is definitely a Blondie."

At this, Iason shook his head. "I'm not following you."

"That special little squeeze you do? He has it."

"That's impossible."

"Improbable is the word you're looking for, since I've experienced it firsthand."

"Well, there must be some other species with that physiology," Iason replied.

"The thing is," Voshka said with a laugh, "we've already matched his genetic profile with the entire Quadrant. He's half Aristian, but the other half is a mystery. And the only genetic code we don't have in the database is from Amoi."

"What is it you want, exactly?" Iason asked, finally.

"I want to send Aranshu's genetic profile to you, and I want you to analyze it against your database and tell me what you find."

Lord Mink shrugged. "I can do that, of course. We won't come up with anything, but I'll do it for you."

"Splendid. I'm relaying the file now."

Iason's screen lit up, confirming receipt of the file.

"Yes, I have it," the Blondie said. "Is there anything else I can help you with?"

"Why, yes, as a matter of fact. You can answer a question for me. Two questions, in fact."

"Yes?"

"The first question is: were you and Raoul ever lovers?"

Iason was so shocked at this that he sat back in his chair, speechless.

"Ah. I think you've answered that for me. Very good. Because I was wondering about this second question, but now I think I'll ask it."

Lord Mink stared at the screen, trying not to tremble. "Yes?"

Voshka laughed softly. "The look on your face just now is priceless. Really. My second question is this: did you kill my brother Anori?"

# Chapter 2 -
# Past Transgressions, Parentage
# & Punishment

IT WAS THE QUESTION IASON HAD BEEN DREADING for years, the very question that he had desperately hoped the Commander would never ask.

And yet, he had asked it.

Iason kept his face neutral, trying not to betray his secret. "Vosh, what kind of question is that? You're asking if I killed your brother while he was staying with me? Of course I didn't. What sort of host would I be, if I had done that?"

The Commander studied him intently, his eyes glimmering. "You're very hard to read, I'll give you that. But I think you're lying to me."

Lord Mink pressed his lips together. "Vosh. After everything we've been through together, you're accusing me of murder?"

Voshka settled back in his chair, crossing his legs. "I think it was a crime of passion. You and Raoul were lovers. He cheated with Anori. You came upon them and, well, I don't know the exact details, but yes, I believe you got your revenge and killed Anori."

Iason lowered his gaze and then looked up at the Commander provocatively. "Vosh…."

"Oh, I see how it is. Now you're using your seductive arts to try and distract me." Voshka laughed softly. "You must take me for a simpleton."

Lord Mink, realizing that he could not win the Commander's trust utilizing sex, fell silent, perplexed.

"Ah. I think I've finally gotten your attention," the Commander noted.

"Commander, you're quite mistaken," Iason insisted.

"Am I?"

"Yes, you are."

Voshka seemed angry. He drummed his fingers on the table next to his chair restlessly, saying nothing.

"Don't tell me you're…going to take some action over this?" the Blondie asked.

"I haven't decided," the Commander answered. "I should send my entire fleet to Amoi and totally destroy your miserable little planet."

"Vosh," Iason laughed.

"I assure you, I do not find the matter amusing."

"But you can't be serious!"

"Were you lovers with Raoul, or not?"

"Yes, but—"

"Then it had to be you," Voshka decided. "I'm ending this call. Consider our friendship also at an end."

"But, Commander—"

"Goodbye, Iason."

With that, the call was terminated. Iason sat for several moments, blinking, and trying to process what had just taken place. Then he sent an urgent outgoing message request to Jupiter.

His message was intercepted by a Sentinel.

"Put me through to Jupiter," Iason demanded.

"What is the nature of your message?" the Sentinel asked.

"We may be at war with Alpha Zen," Lord Mink replied.

❦

YUTAKU SET A BOOK BEFORE AMON, SMILING. "You might find that interesting," he said. "I just finished reading it."

"What is it?" Amon asked.

"It's a book about the Qentu Kings during the Old Age on Amoi."

Amon looked startled, and then carefully picked up the book. "Where did you get this?"

"It's an import from Aristia, actually, oddly enough. You come from a great line."

Amon flipped through the book, and then gazed up at Yutaku, mystified. "Who are you?"

"I told you; I'm Yutaku Iman, your new Master."

"But why would you give me this book?"

"Well, I thought it might be of interest to you," Yutaku answered, frowning. "Was I wrong?"

Amon stared at him for a long moment. "You can't know…what this means to me," he said finally.

"Ah. Very good. I was hoping you would like it."

At that moment the tailor arrived from Eos with clothes for Amon—the only thing that would fit, which was a Blondie's outfit.

"Here," Yutaku said, handing Amon the garment. "The tailor is here to measure you, but you can put this on for now. I'm sure you're anxious to get into something…clean."

Amon took the clothes at first without reply, gazing at them as if in awe. "These aren't pet clothes," he remarked finally.

"No," Yutaku agreed. "There was nothing else that would fit you. It will do for now. You can go to the bath hall to change."

Nodding, Amon got up from the table where he had been sitting and left for the bath hall, taking the garment—and the book—with him.

Yutaku stared after him, frowning. He hated seeing the great Federation leader reduced to a position of subservience. It went against all his principles. Especially now that he had read about the line of great kings Amon was descended from, it seemed ridiculous to call such a man a "pet".

Orin announced the arrival of a visitor—Headmaster Sung.

"Blast," Yutaku said under his breath.

"What was that?" Konami asked, as he strode into the room.

"Oh, nothing," Lord Iman said, smiling politely. "Good to see you, Headmaster. What can I do for you?"

"I just came to see how you are doing with Amon. Has he been much trouble for you?"

"No, surprisingly, he has not," Yutaku answered.

"Really?" Lord Sung seemed dubious.

"Well, initially he might have resisted a bit, but he's beyond that now. He's just in the bath hall, changing, presently."

"What, don't tell me you're letting him go about unshackled!"

"He doesn't seem to need restraints," Yutaku protested.

"Are you mad? He's just waiting for an opportunity to kill you, probably while you're sleeping," the Headmaster retorted.

"Surely not," Yutaku said, frowning. "But I do keep my bedroom door locked."

"I'm glad to hear that, at any rate. And he *is* wearing a D-class pet ring. I made sure of that myself. At least he can't leave the premises."

Yutaku blushed. "Yes."

At that moment, Amon emerged from the bath hall, dressed head to toe in Blondie garb.

"What's this?" Lord Sung demanded. "Why is he wearing Blondie clothes?"

"Oh. Well, nothing else would fit him. The tailor is here, we were just about to measure him for a new wardrobe," Yutaku explained.

"No, no, this won't do at all! No pet wears his Master's clothes!"

"They weren't actually my clothes—"

"Don't argue with me! I'll bring my cane with me next time and give you a few strikes with it! No, have him change out of that outfit at once!"

Yutaku sighed, looking toward Amon and noting that the man looked spectacular in his new clothes, with his unexpected long dark hair. "Amon, go change back into your other clothes," he instructed.

"But you told me to put these on," Amon protested.

"Don't let him talk back to you," the Headmaster hissed. "Discipline him!"

"But I haven't an implement," Yutaku replied.

"Then procure one!"

Yutaku turned to Amon. "Now I'm telling you to take them off," he snapped. "Obey me at once."

The man eyed the Headmaster gloomily and turned on his heel, seeming angry.

"And put him back in chains," Lord Sung commanded.

Yutaku frowned. "Is that really necessary?"

"Absolutely! You can't have him walking about as he pleases until he's perfectly tamed!"

"But he hasn't caused any trouble. Not much, anyway."

"Oh? Has he tried to attack you?"

"Once," Yutaku admitted. "But I restrained him."

Lord Sung sighed loudly. "It's a good thing I came by. I'll wager he had plans for you. He's just pretending to be docile to catch you off-guard, Yutaku."

"Do you really think so?"

"Yes, I do. Believe me, I've seen what this man can do. He is not someone you want to mess around with."

"But it doesn't seem right…."

"Excuse me?"

"I mean, he's descended from the great Qentu kings and all," Yutaku explained. "It doesn't seem right to see him in chains."

The Headmaster stared at him for a moment. "Do I need to remind you of your responsibilities as a Blondie and a Master?"

"No," Yutaku said weakly.

"Then I suggest you do as I say. I'll be returning again to check on your progress. Get a whip or a taming stick. Good afternoon." With that, the Headmaster left the premises.

Yutaku cursed, causing Orin to giggle. He rarely heard his Master use vulgar language.

"Pardon me, Orin," Yutaku said. "I'm not myself at the moment."

"Can I bring you anything, Master?"

"Yes, a scotch would be perfect, thank you."

"Yes, Master."

Yutaku waited impatiently with the tailor for Amon to return to the hall, but the man was slow in coming. When he finally did return, wearing his old clothes, he avoided looking at Yutaku.

"Pet," Yutaku said in a firm voice, "come over here."

Amon reluctantly approached him, a puzzled look in his eyes.

"We're going to measure you now for your wardrobe," Lord Iman explained, and then added, in a softer voice, "I'm sorry about the Headmaster's visit. He can be very…difficult about certain things. You looked quite good in the clothes; they suited you. But, I'm afraid, for reasons I'd rather not get into, the Headmaster thought it was inappropriate for you to be wearing them."

"Because I'm a worthless pet," Amon answered, his eyes glimmering darkly. "Those clothes are for Blondies, like you."

Yutaku hesitated. "I wouldn't put it like that. But yes, those were Blondie clothes. It was my fault; I shouldn't have had you put them on, in the first place. I didn't think it would be such a big issue, but apparently, I was mistaken."

"So you're going to make a wardrobe for me that's appropriate for my status," Amon said, his voice thick with venom.

"Yes, exactly."

"I'd rather die than wear it!"

"Pet, you mustn't say such things."

"Go ahead, put me back in chains. I heard you talking. I know it's what you're going to do."

"Now, Amon, I'm sorry, but, yes, the Headmaster insists you be shackled for a while more. I tried to tell him you were no trouble, but he wouldn't listen to me."

Amon was silent. "Can I keep the book?" he asked, finally.

Yutaku nodded. "Yes, of course. But now I must insist, as soon as we finish measuring you, that we put you back in your manacles."

Surprisingly, Amon did not resist, but allowed the Blondie to measure him and then shackle him to the bed.

"Your scotch, Master," Orin said, arriving, a bit late, with the wanted drink.

"Ah. Very good." Yutaku took a sip and then looked at the clock. "Orin, I'm going to be gone for a few minutes. If you have any trouble, I'll be next door, at Omaki Ghan's villa."

"Yes, Master."

Yutaku drained his scotch and handed the glass back to Orin, and then made his way over to Omaki's villa.

He was relieved when Omaki answered the door himself.

"Lord Ghan, goodness, I wasn't expecting you," Yutaku said anxiously.

"Oh? And who were you expecting to be at my villa?"

"I only meant…where is your attendant?"

"At the hospital presently. What can I do for you?"

"I was wondering if, by any chance, you might have some sort of disciplinary device, such as a whip or a taming stick that you might be inclined to lend me?"

Omaki smiled, putting a hand on his shoulder. "You've come to the right place. Come inside."

Lord Iman followed the Blondie inside the villa, laughing nervously at the image of Iason that was still rotating over the punch bowl in the corner of the room, which apparently Omaki had not dismantled yet after his great bash.

"May I ask what you'll be using the device for?" Omaki asked.

"It's for…well, Headmaster Sung insisted I procure something, to deal with Amon."

"Ah, I see. While normally I would recommend a taming stick, with a man of his size I might go with something a little more robust, like a whip." Lord Ghan led Yutaku into a room that was filled, wall to wall, with all manner of disciplinary objects.

"Goodness," Yutaku laughed. "You certainly are well-stocked."

"I am, indeed," Omaki agreed. He picked out a C-17 kasey whip that had some flexibility to it and made an impressive whishing sound when he whipped it through the air. "This should do nicely," he said. "It has some buffering technology so you won't mar that pretty skin of his, but it has a bite to it, no question. A few strikes with this and he'll be more obedient. Are you having trouble with him?"

"Well, not precisely," Yutaku said.

"No?"

"That is, the Headmaster thinks he should be in chains."

"You mean he's not?"

"He is now, but before, he wasn't, no."

"Do you have any idea what that man did to Iason and Riki?" Omaki asked.

"Not really," Yutaku admitted.

"Let's just say, if he had completed his agenda, I don't think either one of them would be alive right now. He's a dangerous man, Yutaku. Surely the Headmaster warned you about that."

"Yes, he did," Lord Iman agreed. "It's just, I hate seeing him in chains."

"Ah, give it time, give it time," Omaki said, handing him the whip. "You'll come to enjoy the sight of your pet in chains. Use this if necessary."

"Oh, I hope it won't be necessary," Yutaku said, taking the whip gingerly, as though he were afraid to touch it. "I'm only asking for it because the Headmaster insisted."

"You're not going to hold it like that, are you?" Omaki demanded, hands on his hips. "No, no, no. Hold it firmly, with authority! Yes, like that!"

Yutaku gripped the whip in his glove, swishing it through the air a few times.

"That's it! Learn how to make it snap!"

The Blondie practiced for a while, taking Omaki's suggestions and familiarizing himself with the instrument of pain he was going to be taking into his villa. Lord Ghan showed him the settings on the panel which allowed him to increase the intensity of the pain by adding a small level of shock—a feature which Yutaku had absolutely no intention of using, but wanted to be sure he understood how to avoid engaging.

"Thank you, Omaki. I'll return this to you when I…well, I'm not exactly sure when," Lord Iman said.

"It's yours. Keep it. *Use* it," Omaki said, grinning. "Would you like to come sit for a while and have a drink?"

"Oh, no. I've taken enough of your time, as it is. And I need to, that is, I should probably get back. Just in case there's any trouble. With Amon, you see."

"Ah. Then, let me know if you have any other disciplinary needs, or if you find that whip doesn't suit you."

"Will do."

The two of them walked back to the door.

"I don't suppose you've gotten him to perform for you?" Omaki asked, his eyes gleaming.

"What? Oh, no. Not yet."

"Ah, well. That's something to look forward to, isn't it?"

"Yes, I suppose so," Yutaku agreed uncertainly.

Omaki studied him. "You *are* going to make him perform for you, aren't you? That is his duty as your pet. Headmaster Sung will insist on it."

"Yes, well, I hadn't really thought about it."

Omaki put a hand on his shoulder. "Think about it, old friend."

"I will. Thank you," Lord Iman replied.

Jupiter immediately came onscreen. "What do you mean, war?"

Iason sighed. "Voshka Khosi knows about Anori. He just accused me of murdering his brother."

"How could he possibly have known?"

"When Raoul and the others activated Anori's craft in an attempt to rescue me, it triggered an alert on Alpha Zen. Voshka then knew we had lied about the crash, and he pieced together the rest."

"This is a most unfortunate development. We must ready our military at once. Can you not use diplomacy with the man?"

Lord Mink shook his head. "I tried, but failed. He says our friendship is at an end."

"So much for the Trade Agreement," Jupiter said, her aura humming red.

Iason nodded, feeling this was the least of their concerns. He was now not at all sure how Amoi would fare in a full-scale attack from Commander Khosi's air fleet.

"I will make arrangements immediately," Jupiter announced. "Let me know if you learn anything more."

Iason bowed his head, and Jupiter terminated the call. He sat for a moment, thinking about Voshka, and wondering if there was anything he could do to tame the man's fury. Then he remembered the genetic sample for Aranshu the Commander had given him. Although it made no sense, he could at least humor the man and process it through the Amoian database.

He found the file and entered it into the system and was stunned when, immediately, three distinct matches were pulled up from the database.

Three Blondies.

More specifically: Omaki Ghan, Yousi Xuuju, and his own identification: Iason Mink.

Iason was stunned. He ran the file through again, just to be sure, but the results came back just the same. Genetically, as a father, Iason was the greatest Blondie contributor to the code, at

38%, with Omaki at 9% and Yousi at 3%. The other 50% was pure Aristian—the mother.

His mind was a tangle of thoughts. Voshka, certainly, but also the genetic match with Aranshu. The answer to that mystery came to him clear as day—it all went back to the time he, Yousi and Omaki had taken the Aristian virgin some twenty six years before. Apparently, she had conceived, and in the peculiar way of Aristian women, she had utilized the genetic code from more than just one father. All three of them were fathers of Aranshu, hard as that was to believe given the supposed sterility of Blondies, but according to the results, Iason's genetic signature was the largest of the three contributors.

So Iason Mink, a Blondie, was a father—the father of Aranshu, Voshka's pet. He didn't know how to process this information. What did he know of being a father, other than being Guardian to Aki? Besides, Aranshu was a grown man. He wondered if this development could be used at all for leverage with the Commander, although he doubted that Aranshu would be pleased when he learned how his conception took place. If anything, it would probably make Voshka more likely to attack Amoi.

Remembering Aki, Lord Mink hurried to ascertain the boy's whereabouts, assuming he was still at Sir Elusiax's home. The boy was, indeed, there, and requesting to spend the night there with Suuki. So, Iason allowed this and returned home to brood.

"YOU SUMMONED ME?" AERTIS STOOD BEFORE Headmaster Sung's desk, looking a little fearful.

"Yes, sit down, Aertis."

The young Blondie did so, sitting forward in his seat. "Is it about—"

"I've contacted Xanthus Kahn about our…indiscretion. And he's agreed to administer the punishment."

"Oh," Aertis said, looking a little disappointed. "When is it?"

"Tomorrow evening at the seventh hour. Why don't we meet here at, say, one-half chimes before and we can proceed to his villa together."

Aertis nodded, frowning.

"I'm afraid it's too late to back out now. Xanthus knows about us. I wasn't even sure he'd agree to punish us, but he did."

"I understand."

"Prepare yourself. It…won't be pleasant."

"Headmaster, if we're going to be punished anyway…."

Konami held up a hand. "No, Aertis. I must insist. We've let this go too far already."

"But it's not just the sex," Aertis said, lowering his voice. "I have feelings for you."

Lord Sung felt his heart beating faster but he did his best to show no reaction. "I told you before, I do not have feelings for you. I'm sorry if you misunderstood."

The young Jin's eyes blazed. "I don't believe that."

"Believe what you want, then."

"I know we have to be punished. But I don't want this to end."

"Aertis," the Headmaster sighed. "You're being unreasonable."

"And you're being insensitive. I know you have feelings for me. And I know you want me. Right now."

"Lower your voice," Lord Sung hissed. "There are students roaming the halls.

"I don't care. Look. We're going to be punished tomorrow. Why not spend tonight together?" He put a hotel card key on the table. "I rented a room at the Dark Horse. I'll be there at the eighth hour. Come and be with me. For just one more night."

The Headmaster glanced at the card, tempted. One more night in young Jin's arms would be heaven. When he looked at Aertis, the boy was gazing at him with lust in his eyes.

"Aertis," he scolded.

"Just one more night," Aertis whispered. Then he got up and left.

Konami stared at the card he left on the table. Quickly, he scooped it up and put it into a drawer. No, it would be pure folly to engage in another night of carnal pleasures on the eve of their punishment. They would, additionally, be forced to admit the transgression to Xanthus, which would compound their punishment.

He wouldn't go. No, certainly not. Most definitely not.

YOUSI AND OMAKI WERE HOLDING THE ARISTIAN down on the bed. She was gagged. She struggled, but she was no match for two Blondies.

Iason, by some unspoken agreement, was the first to take her. He was so excited, he was trembling.

The woman was beautiful, no question—an exotic pick straight from the shores of Aristia. She was one of Omaki's first acquisitions at the Taming Tower, and the Academy Blondies were anxious to spend their young seed.

It was Iason's first sexual experience. It mattered little that she was a captive—if anything, that only aroused him even more—and the fact that such an act was so expressly forbidden made the whole experience one of the most erotic in his life.

He took hold of her flimsy dress and ripped it open. The woman stilled at this, breathing hard. She was naked beneath the dress, but for a pair of panties, which Iason quickly removed.

Her breasts were full and magnificent. Iason began suckling the nipples, removing one of his gloves. The woman opened her mouth, gasping. Iason used his fingers to ascertain whether she was aroused.

"Is she wet?" Omaki asked, smiling.

"Yes," Iason reported, continuing to fondle her.

"She's not struggling so much now," Yousi remarked.

Iason unfastened his trousers and pulled out his cock. The woman's eyes widened. "Hold her legs open," he commanded.

Yousi and Omaki obliged him, but the woman seemed to have given up her struggle. He put his cock up to her opening and began entering, eliciting a strangled moan from the woman.

Iason's eyes rolled back as he penetrated completely, splitting her open.

DARYL WAITED IMPATIENTLY FOR NEWS ABOUT Katze. When the physician finally came out into the waiting room, he was grim.

"I'm afraid it doesn't look good," he said. " The bullet hit part of his heart. We're doing the best we can, but the injury is serious."

Daryl listened in stunned disbelief. He had been told that all they had to do was get to the hospital, and everything would be fine! Wasn't that was Sarius kept repeating the whole way to the hospital?

"Can I see him?" he asked breathlessly.

"No; he's still in surgery. I just came out to update you."

"But are you saying he could die?" Daryl cried.

The physician nodded. "You have to prepare yourself for that possibility. I'm sorry. We'll try to save him, if we can."

Daryl broke down sobbing, and the others in the waiting room tried to comfort him, but he didn't even hear them. All he knew is that his wonderful Katze, his beloved, was close to death. And Daryl knew that if he lost Katze, he wouldn't want to go on living, either.

LORD MINK COULDN'T SLEEP. HE GOT OUT OF BED, put on a robe, and made his way into the great hall, pouring himself a glass of Red Aristian Emperor wine, and then sat down in his favorite chair by the fire.

He was thinking about Voshka and Aranshu, of course. He hardly knew what to think about either situation.

But even more than this, ironically, Iason brooded over Riki and Ima. He remembered that Riki had lusted over the images of Ima in the contraband pet magazines. He couldn't get the thought out of his mind of the two of them together. He frowned, wondering if Riki had feelings for the pretty little pet.

He would never want to admit it to Riki, but he was relieved that Ima had lost the child. He was horribly jealous of Ima, and she would have always been coming around because of the child. But he was sorry for Riki because he knew the mongrel had wanted it.

Riki woke up and found the bed empty. He sat up, confused. "Iason?"

"In here, love," the Blondie called.

The mongrel got up and went into the great hall, completely naked. Iason smiled at him, patting his lap. "Come sit down."

"Why are you up?" Riki asked, yawning.

"I couldn't sleep."

The mongrel snuggled onto Lord Mink's lap. "Mmmm. You're warm. So what's on your mind? Are you worried about Vosh?"

"I suppose."

"You suppose? That's not what's bothering you?"

Iason fell silent, sipping his wine.

"What, you're not going to tell me?" the mongrel protested.

"It's of no consequence."

"Well, it must be of some consequence if you can't sleep."

The Blondie laughed softly. "It's foolish."

"What is?"

"I'm wondering…if you preferred Ima to me."

Riki laughed. "Is that what you're worried about? Fuck, no. I told you that already. She was nothing."

"But you…kept those photos of her."

"Only because I didn't have any other ones, hardly, until you took even those away."

Iason frowned. "Aren't I satisfying enough for you? Why do you need additional stimulation?"

"Oh, come on. I bet you get off looking at stuff, too. Am I right? Videos or something?"

Iason was silent, remembering the contraband video he and Raoul had watched together, the one where the Master Blondie engaged in sexual congress with a pet.

"In fact, as I recall, you Blondies like to watch."

"You didn't answer my question," Iason answered.

"Because it's a stupid question. Everyone enjoys additional stimulation. It's not that you're not satisfying. It's just good to shake things up every now and then."

"What do you mean, 'shake things up'?"

"You have to ask me that? Don't you Blondies have pairing parties all the time?"

Lord Mink frowned. "That's not the same."

"Isn't it? I thought the whole idea was so you could get off on it."

"Perhaps you're right," Iason conceded, with a sigh.

"What? You mean you're actually agreeing with me for once? Does that mean I can have my magazines back? Or maybe some new ones?"

"No, it does not."

"Sheesh. You're no fun. What if we looked at them together?"

"No, Riki."

"Well, what about we watch a pairing together? Isn't that what you Blondies are supposed to do?"

"I'll think about it," Iason replied.

The mongrel brightened at this. "You will?"

"Yes, in fact, I think there's going to be a few pairings at our next get-together on Jupiter's Eve," Lord Mink said. "I can't remember the precise details."

"Oh yeah," Riki said, remembering. "That's just the day after tomorrow!"

"But are you sure you want me to watch a pairing, Riki?" Iason asked, his eyes gleaming.

"Of course! Why not?"

"You won't be jealous?"

Riki frowned. "I don't think so."

Now Iason whispered in his ear, "You won't be jealous when you see me getting aroused over someone else?"

"Well, when you put it like that…."

Lord Mink laughed softly.

"Are you coming to bed?"

"I don't know if I can sleep."

"I know something that will put you to sleep," Riki whispered seductively.

"Oh, pet," Iason breathed.

"Come on." Riki stood up and held out his hand. "Let's go to bed."

Voshka stood at his window, looking out over the pavilion, his hands clasped behind his back. Aranshu had watched him for some time, being unwilling to disturb him.

The man was angry.

Aranshu knew well enough when his Master was angry, and he knew better than to bother him. He was sure it had to do with the conversation he'd had earlier with the Blondie from Amoi—the one called Iason Mink—and the one Voshka had accused of murdering his brother. Aranshu had heard the whole conversation—only pretending to be asleep.

He remembered well enough the way his Master had broken down over the news that Anori had died. It had been the only time he had ever seen the man cry. Now, he appeared to be convinced that the Blondie had something to do with Anori's death. And knowing the Commander, Aranshu was sure that this would not be the end of the matter.

No, Voshka was scheming something.

Aranshu got dressed quietly, putting on the same outfit he had worn before, as he had no idea what else to wear.

The Commander heard him and turned. "What are you doing?"

"Dressing," Aranshu said.

"But you can't wear that again," Voshka protested.

"I don't have anything else to wear."

The Commander's lip twitched. "Come. We'll find you some suitable clothes in the harem."

"The harem?" Aranshu said, frowning. "Do we have to go back there?"

Voshka gave him a warning look but said nothing.

Aranshu hurriedly finished dressing and followed his Master out of the room, still barefoot. Everywhere they went, people saluted the Commander and gawked at Aranshu, some of them laughing.

Aranshu frowned. "Why are they laughing at me?"

"Because the whole palace knows you were punished yesterday," Voshka replied.

"The whole palace?" Aranshu said, stunned. "Don't they have anything better to gossip about?"

"Surely you haven't forgotten what it's like to live in the palace."

"But this one's so much bigger, I thought…."

"Some things don't change, Aranshu," the Commander said.

"But some things do," Aranshu said glumly, as he saw Velo walking toward them.

"Ah, Velo. Myri Eroni."

Aranshu frowned at this greeting, immediately recognizing the words. My pet.

Velo greeted him with a bow, kissing the Commander's ring.

Aranshu snorted at this.

Voshka shot him an irritated look. "Do you find something amusing?"

For a moment, Aranshu was tempted to give a sarcastic reply, but the look in the man's eyes stayed him. "No, Master," he said meekly. His ass was still killing him from the previous day, and he had no desire to incite Voshka's wrath again.

The Commander noted his submission with a look of pleasure. "Good. It seems you're finally starting to learn your place."

"Yes, Master."

Voshka turned away and spoke to Velo in Alphazenian, causing the man to laugh softly. Aranshu frowned, trying to follow the conversation and wishing he had tried harder to learn the language while he was on the planet before.

Whatever it was they were talking about, Velo seemed pleased about it. He nodded and then made his departure, glancing at Aranshu with a smirk at his lips.

"He's laughing at me," Aranshu complained.

"Don't start, Aranshu."

"What were you talking about?"

"That is between Velo and I."

Furious with this answer, Aranshu fell into a grumpy sulk.

"Are you going to pout?" Voshka asked. "Perhaps I'll have to rethink giving you your reward today."

At this, Aranshu brightened. "What is my reward?"

"Ah, that made a difference in your disposition, didn't it? Perhaps I'll show you now, since we're passing by that way."

"What?" Aranshu asked, puzzled.

"Your rooms. That's your special reward," the Commander said, stopping in front of a set of double doors. The doors opened at Aranshu's approach.

"Welcome, Aranshu," said the overhead voice. Aranshu stopped in his tracks, completely overwhelmed. He had been impressed with Velo's rooms, but these rooms were far bigger and even more magnificent. They were filled with every kind of treasure he could possibly imagine.

Everywhere he looked, he saw something to catch his eye—shells, rocks, gems, flowers, pottery, art, and musical instruments. One entire wall was a window, looking out over the pavilion, with the mountains in the distance. There was a magnificent chandelier hanging from the ceiling, and the room was decorated with several priceless Vergatti vases. An immense bed occupied the center of the room, and on it, Aranshu was pleased to see the same mysterious rotating, floating pillows that had so fascinated him in Velo's bedroom.

There were shelves of golden-bound books—from Aristia, he noted—as well as beautiful objects of art. An open bar was situated near a billiards table, and there were other holographic games in one corner of the room.

One wall had a fountain in it, and another wall boasted a fireplace that was burning brightly with a low fire, the logs crackling and snapping. There were beautiful paintings on both these walls. A third wall was another holographic illusion of a beach, much like he had seen in Velo's room, which reminded him immediately of Aristia, the waves seeming to intrude almost into the very room.

A spiral staircase led to an upper level, where there were more surprises—an indoor garden, a small pond, and a relaxing view of the mountain range in the distance. That level had enormous chairs for sitting, a smaller bar, and a walk-in kitchen, in addition to a grand bath hall. And of course, everywhere he looked there were beautiful decorative objects that looked to have cost a fortune to complete the rooms.

Best of all, there was a giant cylindrical aquarium that went floor to ceiling through both floors like a giant tube and in it were all manner of beautiful, colorful fish and sea creatures—again reminding him of home.

"What do you think?" Voshka asked softly, coming up behind him to whisper in his ear.

"Oh….Master, I—this must have taken you a long time to…to…build," Aranshu said, finally.

"I had a long time to build it. Ten years, to be exact."

"It's—I love it!"

"I'm glad you're pleased."

"I am! I—it's better than Velo's room, even!"

At this, the Commander laughed. "Come. Let's try out the bed, shall we?"

"Are you still angry?"

Voshka look surprised. "How did you know I was angry?"

Aranshu smiled. "Believe me, I know when you're angry."

"I'm not angry at you."

"Well, that's something."

"You're really pleased, then?"

"Master, I—" Aranshu turned to face the Commander, suddenly at a loss for words. "I'm touched that you…saved these rooms for me, all this time."

"Oh, Shu." Voshka looked at him, his eyes glimmering brightly.

Next they were kissing each other as though they had never kissed before. They somehow made their way to the bed, pulling their clothes off each other.

"I'm dying for you," Voshka hissed.

"You don't know how much…I missed this."

"Then why did you not come back?"

Aranshu shook his head. "I was stubborn. I was angry. And then I was…afraid."

The Commander studied him, and then kissed him again. "I never gave up searching for you. I had to have you back in my arms."

"Then why do you still need Velo?" Aranshu whimpered.

"Hush," Voshka said, silencing him with a kiss. "Don't spoil it."

"But you know how jealous I get."

"I do know," the Commander answered, smiling. "It's one of the things I find endearing about you." He traced a finger down Aranshu's chest to his special gland, stroking it provocatively.

Aranshu arched his back, his lips parting. He closed his eyes.

"You enjoy...torturing me," Aranshu accused.

Voshka laughed softly. "I seem to recall it wasn't all torture for you."

"Please let it just be us."

"You know I can't make you that promise."

"Why not?"

"Because of your intractability. I never know when I might need to...discipline you."

"At least promise me you won't bring any of those garland bearers to our bed," Aranshu pleaded.

"Ah, but I happen to adore garland bearers," Voshka whispered, kissing Aranshu's throat, "as you well know."

"Please."

"Hmmm?"

"You're...I'm about to burst."

"Tell me what you want."

"I want you to...love me with your mouth."

Voshka shot him a smile before he moved down between his legs and began servicing him. Aranshu cried out openly, his hands buried in the man's soft, dark hair. He looked down and saw his cock disappearing in the Commander's mouth.

"Holy fuck! Your tongue is pure heaven!"

The Alphazenian loved him slowly, watching his every move. Aranshu was beside himself with pleasure, not even attempting to hide his delight. As the Commander brought him to the brink, Aranshu began panting, then groaning, and finally he let out a long sex-cry as his seed burst forth into the man's mouth.

"You don't know…how much I've missed hearing you cry out like that," Voshka remarked, as he reached for some lubrication on one of the side tables by the bed. He spread the oil onto his cock and for a moment just remained on his knees, looking down at his pet.

"That was…fucking unbelievable," Aranshu whispered.

"Hold your legs apart for me," Voshka commanded.

Aranshu did so, and Voshka immediately plunged inside without prelude, mounting the Aristian full-force.

Aranshu, though surprised, was not hurt by the assault; he accepted the incursion, noting that some things had changed in his physiology in the ten years since he had last been with the Commander.

"Mmmmm," Voshka purred. "You feel perfect, my pet. That's it. Hold your legs wide apart for me."

He began rocking against him, fucking him without restraint.

Aranshu gazed up at the man, stunned by his physical beauty. Had the Commander always been so handsome, so virile? Or was he only now old enough to appreciate it?

"I love you," he said, without thinking.

Voshka slowed his thrusting. "What?"

"Nothing." Aranshu turned his head away.

But the Commander had heard his proclamation and was now seized with an influx of carnal excitement. "Oh, Shu," he said, fucking him harder, "say it again."

Aranshu remained silent.

"Say it!"

"Oh!"

"Now you're gripping me sweetly, Shu," Voshka said through clenched teeth, "say it again so I can hear it while you milk me with your delightful squeeze."

Aranshu looked up at him, trembling. "I love you," he whispered.

"Yes," the Commander hissed, slowing his thrusting as he ejaculated. He closed his eyes, savoring the moment. Then he slowly withdrew and fell back on the bed beside Aranshu. "Come here," he said, opening his arms.

Aranshu snuggled up with the man, feeling strangely happy. For that moment, it didn't matter that he belonged to the Commander, or that he was his pet. Maybe it was because he knew he was where he was meant to be.

AERTIS WAITED AT THE DARK HORSE, FROWNING when the clock chimed eight o'clock. The Headmaster wasn't coming.

Disappointed, he sat on the edge of the bed, wondering what he should do. He was horribly aroused. Perhaps he should watch a holo-flic and then relieve himself. Sighing, he flipped through the booklet of offerings and then ordered a flic of a Headmaster disciplining a student, as this reminded him the most of Konami.

He had just started the holo-flic when the door opened and Lord Sung entered the room.

"You came!" Aertis said, standing up and rushing over to him.

"I shouldn't have," Konami said, though he didn't resist when Aertis began kissing him.

The two of them groped at each other for a few minutes before making their way over to the bed.

"What's this?" Lord Sung asked, motioning to the holo-flic.

"Oh," Aertis blushed. "I thought you weren't coming."

"I see. And this is what you find arousing?"

"It reminded me of you."

"Oh, Aertis," Konami breathed, kissing him again.

"Let's fuck all night," Aertis suggested.

"We really shouldn't," Lord Sung said.

"But now that you're here," Aertis said, unfastening his tunic, "why not make the most of it?"

"Aertis, Aertis. You undo me."

"Must we really submit to the punishment?"

"I'm afraid so."

"But what good will it really do? You know as well as I do we can't stop this now."

Headmaster Konami frowned, wondering if this were true.

RIKI WOKE UP AND THEN GROANED, REALIZING that it was the day he was getting paddled by Heiku Quiahtenon. Iason was already up, having risen hours before.

He got out of bed and padded into the great hall, completely nude.

"Riki," Lord Mink admonished. "I shouldn't have to tell you— go put on some clothes."

"But I'm hungry."

"You heard me."

"I was naked last night and you didn't care."

"Well, this is the day time and I do care, so go get dressed, or shall I be forced to give you a spanking before your punishment today?"

"Sheesh," Riki said, turning around and leaving the great hall. "Somebody is grumpy this morning."

"Riki," Iason sighed, turning his attention then to an article in Tanagura Quarterly. He was absorbed in the article and didn't notice when the mongrel came back into the hall, this time not having brushed his hair, which was sticking out every which way.

"I'm starving. What's for breakfast?" Riki demanded, sitting down at the table.

Iason looked up and saw him and then put down his journal, sighing. "Pet. Did you bother looking in a mirror? Go brush your hair."

"Huh? What's wrong with it?"

"Riki…."

"Why are you on me? Back off, Blondie," the mongrel said, yawning. "Yui! Bring me some coffee."

"Did you hear me, Riki? I told you to go brush your hair!"

"Coming, Sir Riki," Yui said, rushing into the great hall with a warming dome and some coffee.

"Pet, you will not eat until you go brush your hair," Lord Mink said, exasperated.

"What the fuck is your problem?" Riki demanded, munching on a piece of bacon. "I'm, like, dying of hunger, here."

"Riki!" Iason stood up, his journal falling to the floor.

The mongrel looked startled, as though he had no idea why Iason was angry. "What?"

"I told you twice to go brush your hair before you ate breakfast! Do not ignore me!"

"Okay, okay, sheesh. I'll go brush my hair! I don't know what you're making such a big fuss about!" The mongrel got up and stomped dramatically out of the great hall, returning a few minutes later with his hair in order.

"Where's my kiss?" Iason demanded, just as Riki was sitting down.

The mongrel let his head fall down to hit the table, moaning. "I'll never get to eat."

"Oh, very well. I suppose if you're going to be that way about it," Iason said, sounding a little cross.

The mongrel perked up. "Yay! Food!" He immediately began eating, eyeing Iason as he drank his coffee. "I'll give you a kiss in a minute," he promised.

"Never mind."

"No, I want to."

"Well, I don't want it now."

"Fine. Be that way," Riki said, frowning. He slurped his coffee loudly, expecting the Blondie to fuss at him for not drinking his juice first. But Iason remained silent, as though absorbed in his journal article.

The mongrel slurped louder, this time eliciting a glance of disapproval from his Master. "Someone has forgotten how to behave in a civilized fashion at the dining room table."

"Yeah? Well, someone is being a big pain in the ass, per usual."

"Riki!"

"Iason!"

Lord Mink slammed his journal down on the table next to his chair, knocking it over.

"Oh shit," the mongrel said, taking off. He ran out of the great hall, looking behind him to see if Iason was following him, and was surprised when the Blondie managed to catch up with him, grabbing him from behind and putting his arms around him.

Riki giggled. "Shit! You're fast!"

Iason nuzzled against him, kissing his neck. He laughed, too, his laughter soft and low.

"I thought for sure you were going to punish me," the mongrel said.

"Don't you think you deserve to be punished?"

"Hell, no. But you can ravish me."

The Blondie laughed again.

"You're just grumpy because you didn't get your kiss."

"Now I want more than just a kiss."

"I can tell. Your cock is pressing up against my back."

"Let's go to your bedroom," Lord Mink suggested.

"Does that mean I get to be on top?" Riki asked, grinning.

Iason continued to nuzzle and kiss the mongrel on the neck.

"Ahh! That tickles! It's…your hair!"

"Oh, Riki…."

"So, are we going to my room or what?" the mongrel asked.

Lord Mink answered that by picking him up and carrying him into the bedroom.

"Oh, you're in one of *those* moods," Riki remarked.

"Yes," Iason answered, tossing him onto the bed. "Get undressed."

"But you just made me get dressed. Make up your mind, Blondie," Riki teased, taking off his shirt.

Lord Mink continued to stand, watching him.

"What, aren't you going to take off your clothes?"

"I'm in the mood for something different."

"Don't tell me it's going to be like when I first came here. You were always just watching me," Riki protested.

"I want to keep my clothes on, but I want you to take yours off," Iason clarified.

"Why?"

"Because…I said so. Do it."

Riki fumbled with his pants, taking them off. He was now completely naked, having worn no shoes when he went into the great hall.

"Why are you so turned on? We had sex last night—only a few hours ago."

"It must have been the Red Aristian Emperor wine," Iason answered.

"What about it?"

"It's an aphrodisiac."

"It is? No wonder you're always drinking that stuff."

"Lie face down on the bed," Iason commanded.

"Oh, your favorite position!" Riki remembered, tossing him a vial of oil. "You must be feeling kinky."

The Blondie caught the oil with one hand and then took off his glove so he could lubricate himself. He unfastened his trousers and freed his cock but otherwise stayed dressed. After smoothing the oil over his erection, he straddled Riki, pushing his legs together and pinning his wrists to his back. Then he bumped the head of his cock up against Riki's portal until he gained entrance.

The Blondie groaned as he slid inside. This time, surprisingly, Riki did not complain. He made a slight moan, and then turned his head to the side.

"That actually feels good."

"Does it, pet?"

"Yeah. It must be this position."

Iason undulated against him, making a breathy hiss with each thrust.

"Oh yeah. Fuck me, Iason."

"Riki…."

"You like watching your cock disappear up my ass, huh?"

"Pet!"

"Shit! Right there, Iason!"

"Here?" The Blondie asked, thrusting deeply.

"Fuck yeah! Oh shit! I'm gonna come! I'm…coming!"

"Riki, Riki…."

Riki let loose a strangled sex-cry and Iason was right on his heels, unleashing a low moan that was so unearthly it gave the mongrel chills.

"Damn that was awesome," Riki proclaimed. "Now can I finish my breakfast?"

❧

THAT MORNING RIKI WANTED TO KNOW HOW everyone was doing at the hospital—Katze, Ayuda, Odi and Askel. Iason put a call in to Tanagura Medical and found out that they were all stable—except for Katze.

Riki was upset with this news. "What's wrong with him?" he demanded.

"From what I understand, he took an injury to the heart," Iason explained gently.

"Oh, fuck. We have to go visit him!"

"He's not accepting visitors now. He's still in surgery."

"But Daryl will need us—or at least me," Riki protested.

"We can't go to the hospital now, Riki."

"Why not?"

"Because Lord Quiahtenon is coming over to administer your punishment this afternoon."

"Don't we have time to go before that?"

"No."

"Well, that's just fucking great!" Riki exclaimed. "I'll be in no shape to go after that!"

"You knew this was coming," Iason pointed out.

"I know, but that doesn't make it suck any less. I'm going to my room."

"Very well, but I expect you to be cooperative when Heiku arrives."

The mongrel made a face at this, but left the hall without another word.

Iason brooded over Riki's upcoming punishment, allowing himself to think about his pet's transgression with Ima. He found that, when faced with the image of Riki with the pretty female pet, he was exceedingly jealous, so jealous that he could hardly stand it. He was so angry about it that he almost felt like telling Heiku that he would be administering the punishment himself.

When had it happened? It had certainly taken place when Riki had been set free for his week in Ceres. But what night? And what had they done together? The Blondie was consumed with imagining the details of their congress, feeling as though Riki had, somehow, betrayed him. It bothered him more, even, than the thought of him pairing with Guy. At least Guy was male. How could he compete with a female? And suppose...the mongrel actually preferred Ima?

He tortured himself with images of their union, and with the pictures he'd seen of Ima in the magazine Riki had kept—a magazine that Iason now kept in the drawer of his desk and frequently looked at, if only to torment himself.

The girl was beautiful, no question. Of course he could see the appeal. But it made him jealous to no end that Riki had copulated with her. And after everything they had shared together, it made him question whether or not his pet was being genuine in their sessions together. It seemed as though his pleasure was authentic. But suppose Riki was only playing him? After all, he had run away when he had the chance. Maybe he was only waiting for another opportunity to get out from under his control.

But no, that couldn't be right. Riki had declared his love, had he not? Iason had offered him his freedom—and Riki had decided to stay with him. The Blondie closed his eyes, remembering that day and savoring his pet's response to him. No, he wasn't thinking clearly. When they were held captive in Qentu, Riki had stated that he loved him again. So why was he so jealous about something that had happened a long time ago?

He couldn't help it. Whenever he thought of Riki together with Ima, he felt his blood start to boil. He was glad Riki had lost the baby. Otherwise she would have been around, all the time. Now, at least, this punishment session would definitively put an end to their little romance. Heiku would certainly get rid of Ima. And that would be the end of that.

Finally, the new security guard announced that Heiku Quiahtenon had arrived.

"Ah," Iason said from his chair, "Yui, please let him in and see that he gets a drink."

"Yes, Lord Mink," Yui replied, rushing to the door.

Heiku entered, carrying a paddle.

"Would you like a drink, Lord Quiahtenon?" Yui asked.

"Yes, I wouldn't mind something. A brandy, perhaps."

"Yes, Sir."

"You might not have bothered bringing a paddle," Iason said. "I have a very good one you can use."

"Oh? What is it?"

"It's a Z7000 Stinger. It even has holes in it. Would you like to take a look?"

"Goodness, yes. I might have guessed you'd have something top-of-the-line."

"Raoul used it on him and found it to be quite effective."

"Raoul, you say?"

"Yes, after Riki broke a Vergatti vase he had sent me."

Lord Quiahtenon looked horrified. "He really broke a Vergatti?"

"He did indeed. Deliberately, I'm afraid." Iason rose and went over to the cabinet where he kept his disciplinary implements and Riki's golden chains. He retrieved the paddle and handed it to Heiku.

"Oh my," Lord Quiahtenon said, putting his paddle down in the cabinet and taking up the Z7000 Stinger. He cradled it in his hands as though captivated. "Yes, this should do nicely."

"Your brandy, Lord Quiahtenon," Yui said, offering him the wanted drink.

"Ah. Yes." Heiku took the drink and, paddle in hand, looked around. "So, where is he?"

"I imagine he's hiding in his room," Iason replied. "Sit down, please. I'll go retrieve him."

Heiku nodded and Iason went down the west wing to Riki's room. He found the mongrel at the billiards table, playing pool.

"Riki. It's time," Iason said.

"Hold on, I'm in the middle of something."

"Now, Riki."

"But I'm just about to clear the table!"

Iason reached out and seized the pool cue from him, whacking him on the ass with it.

"Yikes!" the mongrel screeched.

"That's just to warm you up. Your punishment is waiting. No more dallying, let's go."

"Oh, all right," Riki sighed, rubbing his ass. "You didn't have to whack me so hard with that!"

"You were ignoring me."

"I don't suppose there's any way I can get out of this?" Riki asked, looking up at Iason with wide eyes.

"No, pet. I told you; my hands are tied. The Code demands that unsanctioned pairings be punished with a minimum of a paddling. You chose to have Heiku administer that. He is here now."

"Well, fuck."

"Clean up your language. We're coming into the presence of an esteemed Blondie," Iason admonished him.

The mongrel sighed, but said nothing.

Lord Mink put his hand on Riki's shoulder as they walked into the great hall, almost as if he expected the mongrel to bolt from the scene.

When Riki saw Heiku holding the Z7000 Stinger, he stopped in his tracks. "Oh, bloody hell," he breathed.

"Riki," Iason scolded.

"Ah. You found him. Good."

Riki frowned. "What about lunch? I never ate."

"You'll take your punishment now, Riki," Iason said. "If you wanted lunch, you should have come for it."

"This day sucks."

"Yes, and I'm afraid it's going to get worse for you, Riki. You took the liberty of having sex with my pet, and now I'm going to make you regret your actions," Lord Quiahtenon announced. He downed his brandy and then set the glass on one of the side tables in the hall.

Riki eyed the paddle, sighing. "All right. Where do you want me?"

"Stand up against this hall pillar. Put your hands up on the pillar."

"I can keep my pants up?" Riki asked, surprised.

"Yes, though it won't help you much, I'm afraid. You're in for quite a paddling."

"Do you have to use that paddle?" Riki asked, frowning. "I really hate that one."

"That only makes me want to use it even more," the Blondie replied. "Now, enough talking. Get into position."

"I don't think you should allow him to keep his pants up," Iason remarked.

"What!" Riki cried.

"No?" Heiku looked toward Lord Mink, reconsidering. "Perhaps you're right. Riki, lower your pants. This will be a bare-bottom paddling."

"Thanks a lot, Master," Riki muttered, as he unzipped his pants.

"What's that?" Lord Mink said sharply.

"Nothing."

"If you have something to say, pet, go ahead and say it."

"I don't have anything to say."

"No? Well, I do," Heiku announced. "Riki, I'm disappointed in you. In fact, I'm quite furious. How dare you take the liberty of pairing with my pet!" He positioned himself behind Riki, who was now standing naked from the waist down, his hands up on one of the hall pillars, his bottom bared for punishment.

"Yes, Riki, you should have known better," Iason chimed in.

"Get on with it, already," Riki groaned.

Heiku looked startled. "Are you dictating to me? How dare you!"

"I mean, I know I fucked up, but I couldn't help it! She's hot as hell! Who wouldn't want to fuck her!"

"Riki," Iason hissed, mortified.

Heiku twirled the paddle in his bionic hand, grinning. "You're piling on the punishment, you know that?" He turned to Iason. "He's not very smart, is he?"

Lord Mink only rolled his eyes to the heavens.

"Very well, if you're so anxious for it, how about this to warm you up?" With that, the Blondie swung the paddle, which met the mongrel's tender flesh with an awesome *WHACK!*

"Yowwww!" Riki cried. "Oh, shit!"

"Are you rethinking your remarks? Perhaps you have an apology in mind now?"

*WHACK!*

"Holy fuck! That thing burns!"

"Riki, watch your mouth," Iason admonished languidly as he sipped his wine.

Heiku swung again, with both hands on the paddle.

*WHACK!*

"I'm sorry I fucked her! I really and for true am!"

*WHACK!*

"Riki, what did I just tell you about your mouth? Stop using vulgar language."

"Oh God, help me!"

*WHACK!*

"Please, Iason, I can't take anymore!"

"Oh, you'll take it. You'll take it until I'm finished giving it," Lord Quiahtenon said, swinging again.

*WHACK!*

Riki began to cry.

*WHACK!*

"Now this is starting to penetrate your consciousness, isn't it?" Heiku taunted. "Perhaps you'll think twice before you do something so foolish again!"

*WHACK!*

"Please stop! I won't…do it again! I won't!"

*WHACK!*

"No, you won't. And I'm going to make sure you never even look at my Ima again."

*WHACK!*

The mongrel let loose an anguished scream.

Heiku's remarks surprised Lord Mink. "Don't tell me you're keeping her?"

"Actually, yes, I am."

*WHACK!*

"Iason! Help me!" Riki begged, tears streaming down his face.

"I only would have thought…after an unsanctioned pairing, you would have wanted to be rid of her," Iason said.

"I could say the same of you," Heiku remarked, his attention momentarily diverted from the paddling.

Lord Mink said nothing. And he was not oblivious to his pet's pleas for help. The truth was, he had initially been quite angry with Riki, and jealous of Ima. He had wanted Riki to suffer a bit, but he was certain that objective had now been achieved. However, he did not want to offend Heiku, by suggesting the punishment be brought to an end. He was hoping the Blondie would be able to see for himself that Riki was completely broken. His bottom was bright red and starting to welt.

"Here's one more for you," Heiku announced, suddenly seeming to lose interest in the discipline session. "Come near my Ima again and I won't be responsible for what I do to you."

*WHACK!*

Riki fell to the floor, sobbing.

Although Iason didn't care for Heiku's threat, he allowed it, simply because he knew the Blondie was angry.

"I trust that satisfied you?" Iason asked politely.

"Oh, yes," Lord Quiahtenon answered, handing him the paddle. "Your pet was punished most thoroughly."

Iason took the paddle and set it on the table by his chair. "Won't you sit down for a while? Another brandy, perhaps?"

"Oh, no. I must get back to the hospital."

"Very well. I will see you again on Jupiter's Eve."

Heiku made a wry face. "Don't remind me. I haven't even started memorizing the Code!"

"Well, you'd best put some time into that. The Headmaster was serious when he said he'd bring his cane again."

"Yes, yes. How could I forget? Although I seemed to notice *you* had no trouble memorizing your sections."

Lord Mink smiled but said nothing.

Heiku nodded at him. "Well, I'm off," he said, as he left the hall.

Riki was still sobbing, curled around the hall pillar.

"I hope this has…taught you never to pair with another pet without my permission," Iason said softly.

"As if you'd ever let me pair with another pet," Riki shot back.

"Riki," Iason sighed.

"Well, it's true. You know you wouldn't."

Lord Mink was silent. He knew Riki's words were true enough, but he couldn't bring himself to admit it. He would never pair Riki with another pet. No, Riki was his, and his alone.

"So, was she worth it?" he asked jealously.

The mongrel was quiet, trying to decide on his answer. He felt like saying *yes*, just to provoke Iason, but given the sorry state of his hind quarters, he forced himself to bite his tongue.

"Oh, you're not going to answer?" the Blondie said, after a moment.

"She was just some stupid girl," Riki sighed.

"I see. So, is that a *no*?"

"Are you going to fucking torment me with retarded questions?" Riki demanded.

"Pet, may I remind you that your punishment is not over until I say it is over. Perhaps you ought to rethink your attitude."

"Oh, fuck. I can't take any more punishment," the mongrel complained.

"Then, I suggest you straighten up."

The mongrel looked perplexed. "What? What am I even doing?"

"You are being *testy* with me, and you know it."

"Testy?" the mongrel blinked. "What does that even mean?"

"You know what I mean."

"I'm just lying here suffering! How is that being testy?"

"Tell me why you did it."

"Why I did…what?"

"Riki!"

"You mean why I fucked her? Because she was there! She was practically naked and she was hot as fuck! What do you want me to say?"

Iason fumed at this answer, saying nothing. Then, "I suppose you…liked her breasts?"

Riki laughed.

"Pet! Do not laugh at me!"

"I'm not laughing at you but that's a stupid question. Have you *seen* her breasts? Of course I liked them! They're big and round and juicy and—"

"Enough."

"Do you want to hear what else I liked?"

"No." Iason stood up. He found he was trembling. He left the great hall and without another word, went into the Master bedroom, the door humming shut behind him.

Riki watched him go, puzzled. His ass felt like it was on fire. He was mad at Iason, at the moment. He decided to go to his room, as it seemed the punishment was finally over. He put on his pants gingerly and then set off for his room.

HEADMASTER KONAMI SUNG WAS GUILT-STRICKEN over his night of sexual congress with Aertis Jin. He knew he should have restrained himself, but, in truth, the experience had been glorious.

But now it was time for their punishment. He picked up Aertis at half past the chimes of six and they made the journey to Xanthus Kahn's seaside villa in silence.

Then, "I don't regret anything," Aertis finally proclaimed.

"Hush," Lord Sung said, giving him a warning look.

"And I don't think I can stop. I don't care what he does to us tonight."

"You won't feel the same way in a few hours," Konami remarked.

"I know you have feelings for me."

Konami was silent. He did have feelings for the young Jin, but he didn't want to encourage the Blondie. He was determined that this punishment session would put an end to their affair.

"Aren't you going to say anything?" Aertis pressed.

"I've told you before, I have no feelings for you," the Headmaster lied. "This was all about physical pleasure."

"I don't believe you."

"I can't help that."

"Do you know why? Because you're a man of principles. You wouldn't just have sex for pure pleasure. You would only cross that line if your heart somehow got involved."

Konami sighed, pulling into Xanthus Kahn's driveway. "We're here," he announced.

"Give me a kiss before we go inside."

"No."

"Please?"

"No, Aertis. I must insist. We are here to be punished."

Aertis frowned. "Well, for the record, I love you, Konami."

Lord Sung stared at the steering bar, saying nothing. Then, "Let's go." He opened the door and got out.

Aertis joined him and they made their way up to the villa. The door opened even before they had a chance to sound the chimes, and Xanthus' attendant, Toris, admitted them into the villa.

"Master Xanthus is waiting for you downstairs," he instructed, pointing to the door that led to the man's disciplinary chambers.

Konami nodded, and he and Aertis slowly made their way down the stairs. They stopped when they reached the room at the bottom of the stairs, horrified.

It was definitely the room of a disciplinarian. The walls were covered with implements of every kind—paddles, whips, straps, canes—as well as ropes and other binding instruments. There were T-stands and other restraining devices in the corners of the room.

Xanthus was standing in the middle of the room, a cane in his hand. Behind him was a restraining bench.

Konami breathed a sigh of relief. So. They were only to be caned—not whipped.

"You think I'm going to be easy on you?" Xanthus asked, as if reading his thoughts. "I'll wager you'll feel every one of these strikes."

Lord Sung nodded. "I'm sure we will. I'm only grateful you spared us the whip."

"I considered the whip. Indeed, I did. And—listen carefully— if you come to me again for punishment, I *will* use the whip. I must say I am completely shocked at the nature of your indiscretion. You, Headmaster, of all people! You should be ashamed!"

"I am," Konami admitted, hanging his head.

"And you, Aertis," Xanthus said, pointing the cane directly at the young Jin, "are you not the star student at the Academy? How could you let something like this interfere with your career?"

"I'm sorry, Sir," Aertis murmured, his cheeks flushing pink.

"Apologies aren't enough. At least you had the decency to seek out discipline for your transgression. Perhaps—and I should hope—you'll think twice before you even look at each other, after tonight."

Konami and Aertis both nodded.

"Xanthus," Lord Sung began.

"Yes?"

The Headmaster opened his mouth, but found that he couldn't quite confess to their tryst the night before. He stepped forward. "I'll go first."

"Very well. Then take off your trousers, your boots, and your cape. I'll be administering this cane on your bare backside."

At this, the Headmaster hesitated. "Surely not?"

"Obey me at once!" Xanthus shouted. "Humiliation is part of your punishment!"

Konami frowned, but removed his cape and then slid off his boots. Next he took off his trousers, his face reddening.

Xanthus pointed to a reclining bench that was angled at about 50 degrees. "Lie on this bench, your hands on the bars below."

The Headmaster obeyed, and was a little distressed when he felt Xanthus manacle his ankles and wrists to the bench. "Is this really necessary?" he asked.

"This is so you can't move out of position until I'm through with you," Xanthus clarified. "Konami Sung, you are being punished for a most egregious offense. You chose to pair with a student, something that is expressly forbidden by the Code of Conduct at the Academy. Therefore I am going to answer you appropriately. May this punishment work to deter you from future such encounters."

With that, Xanthus began his punishment. He brought the cane down, hard, on the Headmaster's buttocks.

Konami was surprised at the brutality of the cane and cried out with the first strike. When Xanthus continued to rain down strike after strike, he lost all sense of composure. Not since he was a child could he remember experiencing anything so painful—and not even then. There was nothing to compare to the burning sensation of the cane on his backside—and he was broken from almost the very start.

Aertis watched in dismay, his heart sinking. He was terrified for his turn under the cane, but more than this, he was worried that after such a beating, the Headmaster truly *would* avoid him, in the future.

And he couldn't stand for that.

No, he knew he was in love with Lord Sung.

RIKI GOT TIRED OF WAITING IN HIS ROOM, SURPRISED when Iason didn't call for him. His ass was killing him, but he decided there wasn't anything he could do about it.

So, he went looking for the Blondie, stunned to find him still in his bedroom. He went into the room, frowning. "Why are you still in bed?"

"I have a headache," Iason replied.

"Want me to rub out your shoulders for you?"

"Yes, love, that would be perfect."

"Take off your clothes," Riki commanded.

Iason obeyed, stripping down to nothing. The mongrel straddled him, pouring massage oil on his back and rubbing it in to work out all the kinks in his muscles.

The Blondie moaned. "That's heavenly, pet."

"We need to do something about these headaches," Riki said. "What brought this one on?"

"Don't know."

"You must have *some* idea."

"Mmmm. That feels good, Riki."

"If it's because of what I said about Ima, I was just shitting you. I was mad."

"Is that so?" Iason opened his eyes at this.

"Yeah. I didn't care much for Ima," Riki lied.

"Truly, pet?"

"Yeah, she was too curvy. It took me forever to come."

"Are you just saying that?" Iason demanded.

"No. I prefer you." This much, at least, was true.

"Oh, Riki," Iason sighed, relieved. "I've been so worried about that. I keep thinking…that perhaps you…preferred her, to me."

"Nah," the mongrel said. "She's just some tramp."

"But you wanted her baby."

"I would have felt that way about anyone," Riki said. "I just wanted to be a father."

"Riki, I have to tell you something."

"Yeah?"

The Blondie was silent for a moment. Then, "As it turns out, *I* am a father."

Riki frowned. "What do you mean? Aren't you Blondies, like, sterile?"

"So we thought. But when I spoke to Voshka, he sent me the genetic sample of his pet, Aranshu. I ran it through our system, and it happens that I am one of the fathers."

"*One* of the fathers? How can there be more than one father?"

"Aranshu is part Aristian. His mother was Aristian. Aristians can…conceive with multiple partners."

"Who are the other fathers?" Riki asked.

"Omaki and Yousi."

"So what…the three of you gang-raped some Aristian years ago or something?" Riki guessed.

Iason nodded. "Something like."

"And you're really a father?"

"Yes."

"Does he know?"

"Not yet. I haven't decided whether to tell Voshka about it or not."

"I see. No wonder you got a headache."

"But your hands are heavenly, pet."

"Don't you want to meet him? I mean, he's your son and all."

Iason thought about this for a moment. "It's true that I don't like the idea of him being a pet," he admitted. "I'd prefer if he came here, to Eos."

"Oh, I see. It's okay for *me* to be a pet, but not your son."

"I didn't mean it that way, Riki."

"How exactly did you mean it, then?"

The Blondie frowned, unsure how to answer.

"Gotcha, didn't I?" the mongrel said triumphantly. "Now I know what you really think of pets."

"Riki," Iason sighed.

"It's too late to back-peddle now. It's already out there. Anyway, I doubt Voshka is going to give up his precious pet for you. He's pretty mad at you right now."

"Yes," the Blondie agreed. "That's why I'm not sure I should even tell him."

"Still, it seems like Aranshu has a right to know."

"I don't see how that's possible, unless there's a way I could contact him privately. But I don't think he'll be too happy when he learns about how he was conceived."

"True," Riki agreed. "So you really did that? Gang-raped some Aristian?"

"We were young and foolish," Iason replied with a sigh. "But yes, we did."

"You're full of secrets, Iason," Riki remarked. "I wonder what else you're hiding from me?"

"Oh, right there, love. You've found a knot."

"I feel it. You're…mysterious, you know that?"

"Hmmm?"

"I mean, just when I think I know you, you tell me something like this. I kinda can't believe you'd do something like that."

"She was very beautiful," Iason answered, "if that makes any difference. It was my first sexual experience."

"Your first? You Blondies are just…weird."

"Riki?"

"Yeah?"

"Did you really mean what you said about Ima? That you didn't care much for her?"

"Yes," the mongrel answered. He knew it was a lie, but one that Iason desperately needed to hear. "How's your headache?"

"Much better."

"Good. Can we go to the hospital? I'm worried about Katze and the others."

"I suppose so. We should probably take food for the attendants."

"Yeah, that's a good idea. Can I have an O-3 for my ass?"

"I think you know the answer to that, Riki," Iason replied.

"Well, it couldn't hurt to ask," the mongrel replied, grinning.

## Chapter 3 -
## What the Heart Says

THE STARS BURNED BRIGHT IN THE TANAGURAN NIGHT sky. Even the lights of the city could not diminish their illumination, and they glistened like Gardanian diamonds in the heavens.

Iason was out in the garden, enjoying the view, for he loved looking at the stars. But the Blondie was brooding. He knew Riki was troubled in spirit, and this made him troubled, as well.

After their ordeal at Minas Qentu, there was such a strong bond between Iason and Riki that each became very much attuned to the moods of the other. When one of them was down, the other knew right away; whether it was Agatha's halo or just a newborn closeness that had drawn them together, it was hard to say, but their souls were intertwined in a way that could never be disentangled again.

And so, when Riki began feeling out of sorts after the loss of his baby, Iason knew, even when the mongrel refused to say anything about it. He knew, just by the look in his eyes, by the slight tremble in his voice, by the hesitation in his replies.

He knew because he loved him.

Riki was hurting.

Lord Mink sighed, wondering what he could do. He finally got up and went looking for the mongrel and found him in his rooms, playing pool.

"You've been aloof lately," he said softly, watching him play for a moment.

"Have I?" Riki aimed at a difficult shot, and nailed it, sending two balls into the side pockets.

"Yes. I was wondering if…there was something on your mind."

"Nothing in particular," Riki answered.

"Hmmm."

"I mean, I'm a little bored. I'd like to go to Midas and visit my friends."

Iason frowned. "I told you, Riki, that's too dangerous. Have your friends come here."

"It's hard for them to get into the city."

"I'll fetch them, then."

"But I don't really want to bring them here."

"Why not?"

"Because," Riki said, blinking, and then turning away, "you wouldn't understand."

"You don't want them to see you with me? As your pet?" Lord Mink guessed.

"Yeah. That's it."

"But you *are* my pet. Surely, they know that."

"I know, but I don't want to rub their noses in it."

Iason sighed. "Don't you think they would be impressed with your place here? You have your own rooms, your own bar— anything you want, you just have to ask for it."

The mongrel shrugged. "They might be impressed. I don't know. I just would rather go into Midas."

"And I told you, *no*."

"Geez, loosen the leash a bit, why don't ya," Riki grumbled, making another outrageous shot that cleared the table.

"You can hardly expect me to let you go bandying about after what happened at Qentu," Lord Mink remarked.

"Bandying about? I wasn't going to go *bandying* about. I just wanted to go into Midas like I used to."

"I'm not comfortable with you going."

Riki sighed loudly. "Whatever."

The Blondie looked put out by this. "I want you to be happy, Riki."

"Sure ya do."

"Riki," Iason scolded, frowning.

Riki laughed. "What? I'm just being real."

"Is that what this is all really about? That I won't let you go into Midas?"

The mongrel was quiet for a moment. He put down his cue. "Not exactly."

"What is it, then?"

Riki stared at him bleakly, seeming hurt. "Don't you know, Iason?"

At this, the great Blondie softened. Now they were finally getting to it. "Your child?" he asked finally.

Riki stood for a moment as if transfixed. "Yeah. My child."

"So you've been brooding all this time about it?" Iason asked.

"Brooding? That's not the word I'd use."

Lord Mink frowned, studying him. "You're sad about it?"

"Yeah. You could say that. I'm sad."

"I'm sorry, Riki. I didn't realize it meant that much to you."

"Well, it did. I thought I was going to be a father."

"You can still be like a father—to Aki," Iason pointed out.

"I suppose," Riki agreed.

"I can't stand to see you sad," the Blondie said. "I wish there was something I could do."

"Yeah, well. There isn't so…don't worry about it. Iason?

"Yes?"

"I hope you don't mind, but I'd like to be alone for a while."

Lord Mink frowned again, unhappy with this turn of the conversation. Never before had Riki asked him to leave, but he could see that the mongrel was on the verge of tears, so he respected his request and withdrew, retreating to the great hall.

The Blondie, of course, brooded over the matter. Yui brought him some wine, which he took gratefully.

"I have some news from the hospital," Yui announced.

"Yes?"

"Katze is out of surgery. They said it went well."

"I'm glad to hear it. And the others?"

"Askel, Ayuda and Odi should be home soon, if all continues to go well," Yui reported.

"Excellent. Thank you, Yui. Any word on Tai and Toma?"

"They are both still at the hospital, along with Freyn. Should I have them report back to the penthouse?"

"No," Iason answered, after a moment. "Let them stay, if you don't mind serving me, Yui?"

"I don't mind," Yui answered. "Master Raoul asked me to help out however I could."

"I appreciate that. I'm sure you're…missing him."

"Yes," Yui agreed uncertainly. "Well, I'd best check on dinner."

Iason nodded, and then thought about Riki's situation again. If only he could think of something that might help lift his spirits.

Suddenly, he thought of a possible solution. One that might make a difference in how Riki felt about things.

He put in a call to Megala Chi.

"Yes?" Lord Chi answered.

"Sorry to bother you, as I know you have many projects," Iason began, "but I have another one for you that I'd like you to begin right away. I'll pay top dollar for it."

"Oh? And what would that be?"

"A very large-scale Orphanage in Midas," Iason answered.

"An Orphanage?" Megala repeated, sounding less enthusiastic.

"This won't be just any Orphanage. This will be the sort of place that will make children want to become orphans," the Blondie explained.

"Ah, I see! Something state-of-the-art, then?"

"Yes, yes. Be creative with it. With slides everywhere. There must be slides. And rides. Make it a wonderland for children. An adventure-house. Do you see what I'm getting at?"

"I'm beginning to see it," Lord Chi exclaimed. "It will be astonishing!"

"I trust you completely to the design. How quickly can you make it?"

"Oh, er…even if I put it on the fast track, it will take at least a month."

"A month! Oh dear. I was hoping to show something to Riki right away."

"Well, I can't make something pop out of thin air," Megala protested, laughing.

"No, of course not," Iason agreed. "It's just…well, I suppose that will have to do."

"You could always buy one of the posh hotels in Midas and temporarily house the children there," Lord Chi suggested.

"Megala, that's brilliant!" Iason exclaimed. "That's exactly what I'll do. Thank you for the idea."

"Certainly. I'll get to work on the plans right away."

Iason disconnected the call and felt very pleased with the matter. The Orphanage was something Riki had asked him for years ago and he had meant to make good on that promise long before, but had never gotten around to it.

He made a few calls and finally came to an arrangement with Kobin Nu, who owned the Golden Suites in Midas, an immense, luxurious hotel. Although Kobin was reluctant to part with his enterprise, Iason offered him such a staggering amount of credits for the place that he could hardly refuse, especially when he heard what the Blondie was planning to do with the place.

"I need the lots surrounding the hotel as well," Iason explained. "I'll be expanding the hotel to accommodate a grand Orphanage, one that's more on the lines of an amusement park than a typical Orphanage. Megala Chi is going to be the architect."

"What a splendid idea," Lord Nu replied. "You should be able to acquire those lots easily enough, with your credit line."

"It's a surprise for Riki," Iason answered. "He asked me to build one a long time ago in Midas for the orphans there. It's a promise that's long overdue."

"I must say, you certainly spoil that pet of yours, Iason," Kobin laughed. "Though after what he did for you at the Public Whippings, I suppose he deserves it."

"That he does," Lord Mink agreed.

"When are you going to open the Orphanage?"

"Just as soon as I can procure the children and attendants to care for them," the Blondie replied. "I want to move quickly on this."

"Well, the hotel is now officially yours. I just got your relay of credits—thank you very much."

"Then, good evening."

"Good evening to you," Lord Nu replied.

Satisfied that all was going as planned, Iason breathed a sigh of relief. He had one part of the surprise underway. Now for the second part.

"Yui," Iason called.

"Yes, Lord Mink?"

"I'm going down to the pavilion. I'll be back before dinner."

Yui nodded, wondering why the Blondie was going out. "Is there something I can get for you?"

"No. I'll just be a few minutes. If Riki asks where I am, tell him I had to run a quick errand."

"Yes, Sir."

Then, with a mysterious smile, Lord Mink left the penthouse.

"RIKI," IASON CALLED OVER THE intercom speaker.

"Yeah?" the mongrel answered from his room.

"Can you come here for a moment?"

There was a slight pause. "I suppose."

Iason waited in the great hall for Riki to arrive, trying hard not to smile. When the mongrel came into the hall and saw the huge gift on the floor, he stopped.

"What's this?" he asked.

"What does it look like? It's a gift. For you."

"For me?" The mongrel considered the box, his eyes wide. "It's...moving."

"Perhaps you'd better open it," Iason suggested.

A pitiful, muffled whine could be heard emanating from the box.

Riki shook his head. "Don't tell me it's a...."

"Open it!"

The mongrel opened the top of the box, and out jumped a fluffy grey and white puppy. He promptly licked Riki on the hand.

"A puppy!" Riki exclaimed.

"Do you like it?"

"I fucking love it! You really bought me a puppy, Iason?"

The Blondie nodded. "I did."

Stunned, Riki stood motionless for a moment, trying to fight back tears. For the Blondie to purchase a real pet—especially now, when he was grieving so much over the loss of his baby, was touching. He couldn't remember Iason ever doing such a thing before. It was like somehow the Blondie had looked into his heart and knew what he needed to heal.

Sometimes Iason really surprised him. This was one of those moments. Riki laughed at the puppy's antics, then wiped the tears from his eyes.

"This is...like...the best present ever," he avowed.

"But this is only part of your surprise," Iason answered.

"Part of it?"

"Yes. But you'll have to wait until after dinner for the other part."

"That's okay. I'm really hungry," the mongrel announced, much to Iason's relief. After days of only picking at his food, it seemed Riki finally had his appetite back.

They enjoyed a quiet dinner, just the two of them—for Aki was visiting with Suuki, and everyone else was at the hospital, except for the new bodyguards. Yui attended them at the table, refusing to sit down with them when Iason asked if he would like to join them. They laughed at the puppy, who scampered about the penthouse and knocked over a stack of journals.

"What are you going to name him?" Iason asked.

"Ios," Riki answered, pointing out the window at the twin moon which hung low in the sky. "I'll always remember this night, and how our souls are intertwined like…like…."

"Like Ios and Erphanes?" Lord Mink finished, eyes shining with love.

"Yes."

"That's beautiful, Riki," Iason praised. "Ios is a wonderful name, and it's quite fitting. It means Gift of Love. And I do love you, Riki. With all my heart I love you."

"Shit," the mongrel said, wiping his eyes again. "You're making me cry."

"Are you finished eating?" Iason asked, smiling mysteriously.

"Yes."

"Then, let's go."

"Where are we going?"

"You'll know soon enough," the Blondie replied.

IASON'S SLEEK HOVERCRAFT WAS IN GROUND MODE, but no less dazzling to the eye. They were alone. Although Iason's bodyguards had been against their going out without armed guards, Iason didn't want to spoil the moment with additional company. Besides, he had a laser gun with him.

As he pulled in front of the Golden Suites in Midas, Riki stared out the window in wonder at all the people who stopped to look at his fancy vehicle.

"What are we doing here?" he wondered aloud.

"Take a look," Iason replied.

"It's the Golden Suites," Riki said, shrugging.

"Not anymore. As of today, I officially own the property. This is the site for your new Orphanage, Riki. The one you asked me to build."

Riki stared back in disbelief, saying nothing.

"Of course, this is just part of the facility. I've acquired the lots surrounding the hotel and Megala Chi will be designing a fantastic building especially for children," Iason continued. "It should be quite...spectacular, when it's finished."

The mongrel shook his head. "You...you did this for me?"

"Yes, Riki. I know you wanted it."

"This is exactly what I wanted," Riki whispered. "I can't believe you really did it!"

"I'm...glad you're pleased," Iason said softly.

"I'm more than pleased, I'm fucking thrilled beyond words! Iason, this is...unbelievably awesome! This is the best gift you could have ever given me. This, and the puppy, you...you really surprised me today."

"I want to make you happy, Riki," Lord Mink said, a little sadly.

"Well, you just did. You made me so happy, Iason! I can't wait to see the faces on those little kids when we find them and tell them they don't have to live on the streets anymore!"

"What?" the Blondie said, his smile fading. "What do you mean, *find* them? Won't they all be at the Midas Orphanage?"

Riki blinked. "Iason. You don't really think those are all the orphans of Midas, do you?"

"Surely you're not saying...."

The mongrel nodded. "The kids I'm talking about live on the streets of Midas."

"Good heavens! But why wouldn't they be at the Midas Orphanage?"

Riki laughed. "Because the Midas Orphanage is something straight out of hell. And because it's full."

"Do you mean to tell me there are little children living on the streets right now?" Iason asked rather endearingly, seeming genuinely shocked.

"You mean you didn't really know?"

"Of course I didn't know!"

"So. You really *would* have done something about it," Riki noted quietly.

The Blondie was silent for a moment, realizing that, perhaps, in all fairness, before Riki came to live with him, he simply would not have cared if there were mongrel children living on the streets. Like all Elites, he had been bred with a disdain for mongrels. But Riki had changed all that for him. He no longer felt any disdain— only love. And loving Riki had opened his eyes to the humanity of all mongrels.

Now, at any rate, it came to him as a revelation of complete horror that there were orphan children living on the streets of Midas.

"How many are there?" he asked breathlessly.

"I don't know. Thousands, probably."

"Thousands!" Iason looked at the hotel and immediately realized the facility would not be enough. With determination, he made up his mind. "This will be the first of many, Riki. We'll build as many Orphanages as it takes until every last child is off the streets of Midas."

Riki brightened. "Do you mean that?"

"Yes. I promise."

"Oh, Iason. That's about the…sweetest thing you've ever said to me," Riki said, his voice starting to break.

"I'm sorry I didn't do this sooner, Riki," the Blondie answered. "I just didn't know."

"It's okay. I can see that you care. That…means a lot, to me."

"I do care. No child should be on the streets."

"I'm with you on that. Iason?"

"Yes?"

"This is almost like…you're letting me be a father. To countless children without one. I can't thank you enough for it. And the puppy—I love the puppy, too, but this really means something to me."

"Oh, Riki. I wanted so much to help you. I—"

But Riki, for once, had initiated a kiss, and the Blondie was silenced. That night, in front of the Golden Suites of Midas, Iason and Riki came to a new level of understanding in their relationship. One that wasn't based on authority or discipline or taming, but simply on love. The Blondie knew Riki was hurting and had done what he could to help. And Riki, in return, loved Iason for it.

"Can we get a room here?" Riki asked, finally breaking away after the two of them had been kissing for quite a while. "I can't wait until we get back home."

"I don't see why not," the Blondie replied, smiling. He was enjoying Riki's enthusiasm. "After all, I own the place."

"We can get the best room!" Riki proclaimed.

"If it's not already taken," Iason warned. "After all, there are still guests in the hotel."

"Oh. Well, as long as we get *some* kind of room, and fast. I want to love you tonight, Iason."

The Blondie needed no additional persuasion. They exited the vehicle and made their way inside the hotel, where they were immediately greeted by the hotel staff, who looked somewhat alarmed to see the Blondie.

"Lord Mink! We weren't expecting you until tomorrow. We still have guests in the building."

"Yes, yes. I'm not here to boot anyone out. I just wondered if perhaps you had a spare room I could stay in tonight with my pet?"

"Oh! But of course, Sir! Would you like the Ambassador's Suite?"

"If it's available."

"It is, Lord Mink. It's, ah, on the top floor, of course. If you'll just put your hand on this screen, here, the door will be programmed to open for you."

Lord Mink pressed his hand against the green screen, and with an accompanying ding! that indicated his signature had been registered, he was entered into the system.

"We've programmed you to automatically have entry to all doors in the building," the clerk added. "I'm assuming that pleases you."

"Yes, it does," Iason replied, "but put my pet, Riki, in the system, too."

"For all doors?" the attended repeated, blinking uncertainly.

"Yes. Complete access."

"Yes, Sir." The attendant turned to Riki. "Place your hand on this screen."

Riki did so, and he was likewise entered into the security system.

The mongrel grinned. "Cool."

"Is there something else?" Iason asked, when the attendant continued to stare at him.

"No, er, that is, Lord Mink, I hope you don't mind me asking, but is it true you're going to transform the hotel into an Orphanage?"

"Yes, it's true. Come, Riki."

"If I might say so, that's very noble of you," the attendant called after them.

Iason only nodded slightly. He didn't like being praised for the Orphanage; after all, it was Riki's idea, not his. He frowned. How was he going to avoid taking all the credit for the enterprise?

Then, an idea came to him. Of course. He should have thought of it before!

"What are you smiling about?" Riki demanded.

"Hmmm? Oh, nothing worth mentioning."

"We're on the top floor! Woo hoo! The penthouse again!" Riki exclaimed, punching the top button on the elevator. He looked around the golden elevator, whistling. "Wow, this place is posh."

"Will it do for the Orphanage?"

"Are you kidding? It'll be paradise!"

"I have great ideas for the additions to the Orphanage," the Blondie said. "It will have lots of slides and rides in it, like an amusement park or a playground. Very experimental design-wise."

"That sounds awesome, Iason. I can't wait to see the blueprints."

"We should have those within the week."

The elevator door opened and directly ahead of them was the door to the Ambassador's Suite, which took up the entire floor.

"Can I open the door?" Riki asked, not waiting for a reply and just heading toward the door.

"Of course, my love."

The mongrel took hold of the handle. There was a tiny *beep beep beep* as the system recognized his signature and the door bolts unlocked with an accompanying click.

Riki opened the door and stepped inside. "Woah," he said, stopping in the doorway and just looking around. "This place is amazing!"

The room was decorated in a very baroque style, with exquisite scrolling details on all the furniture, and a huge chandelier hanging from the ceiling. The feet of the chairs looked like lion's paws, and the tables were trimmed in gold.

"Wow, look at this bed!" Riki announced, jumping onto the huge King-sized bed that graced one of the rooms. The room had an immense window with a view of Midas, Tanagura in the distance beyond the bridges that connected the two cities. "This is perfect for tonight."

"Why is it perfect, Riki?" Iason asked, walking slowly into the room.

"Because I wanted tonight to be special. Look! There's champagne!" Riki pointed to the bottle of champagne that was left on one of the tables, along with two glasses.

"It's a good year, too," Lord Mink remarked, taking a closer look at the bottle. "Kobin certainly spared no expense for his Ambassador's Suite."

"Let's open it and have some. I want to make a toast," Riki announced.

"To what, Riki?" Iason asked, as he opened the bottle. The cork flew out with a loud pop! and champagne immediately started coming out of the bottle.

They both laughed as the Blondie tried to pour it into the glasses.

"A toast to you, and to this magnificent Orphanage!"

"Very well; but let's make it to us and the Orphanage."

"Okay," Riki agreed.

"To us and the Orphanage!" they both toasted, clinking their glasses together and then sipping the bubbling brew.

"Mmmmm! It's good! It tickles my nose!"

The Blondie laughed and sipped his champagne slowly.

"From here, Tanagura looks so far away," Riki remarked, looking out the window. "This is the view I had growing up—though, granted, not from the penthouse floor. It seems strange to be back in Midas tonight. I mean, and not with my friends or anything."

Iason frowned. "Are you sure you want to be here with me?"

The mongrel looked surprised. "Of course I'm sure. That isn't what I meant. Yes, I especially want to be with you tonight. I want to love you tonight, Iason. It's just ironic that it's here, in Midas. But in a way, it's perfect."

The Blondie looked out the window at the view, quiet.

"Let's get on the bed," Riki suggested.

They both climbed onto the immense bed after putting their champagne aside, and for a long time they just held each other.

"This is nice," the mongrel said, gathering a strand of Iason's hair and bringing it up to his nose. "Your hair always smells so good."

"Oh, Riki," Iason said, holding him tighter.

"You know, I understand something now. You get me. I didn't know you really did, until today. When you bought me that puppy and made the promise to build the Orphanages, I realized you knew what I was feeling, and you wanted to do something about it. You don't just say, 'I wish I could help,' and then do nothing. You do something. I love that about you."

"It's because I love you, Riki," the Blondie whispered.

"I know. And Iason, for the record, I love you, too."

"Do you really, Riki?"

"I just said I did, didn't I?" Riki got up and straddled the Blondie, looking down at him with an impish smile. "Yeah, I love you. I've loved you for a long, long time. Sheesh, don't you know that?"

"How long?"

"Since almost the very beginning. Since before I wanted to, that's for sure. You got into my heart and I couldn't get you out."

Iason frowned. "Did you want to get me out?"

"At first, maybe. You know how it was. I didn't exactly come with you out of my own free will. But with time, all that changed. And it's different now. I can tell…you respect me. I didn't think you did, before."

Lord Mink was quiet for a moment. "I've loved you from almost the very beginning, as well. Even though I told myself I shouldn't. Even though I knew it could cost me…well…almost everything. And Riki, when I found out what you did for me at the Public Whippings, I was so…moved in my spirit. I thought then, maybe you did love me, too."

"Of course I love you."

"You don't always say it. In fact, you rarely say it."

"I know I don't. I should. I just figured…you knew."

"I like to hear it," Iason admitted.

"If I say it too much, it will lose its meaning," Riki argued.

"I know," the Blondie agreed. "But I'd still like to hear it, every once in a while."

"Well, I just told you, didn't I?"

"Say it again," Iason pleaded.

Riki laughed. "You mean, right now?"

"Yes. Tell me what your heart says."

"My heart says that I love you. That I've never loved anyone, the way I love you. That even though sometimes you make me angry, I forgive you, because I know you're trying your best. You're only doing what you've been taught. But you've changed, Iason. You've become…easier to love. Like today, for instance. What you did for me, because you knew I was hurting, because you knew I wanted to be a father—what could be more perfect? You gave me a puppy and an Orphanage. Now I'll be a father to countless children. That makes me so happy. I can't even really express to you, how happy that makes me. It's something that's always bothered me, the orphans of Midas. And now you're doing something about it, for me. I love you for it, and I love you, Iason. I love you so much, sometimes it hurts."

"Riki, Riki," Iason murmured, pulling him close. "Kiss me."

The mongrel repositioned himself and they began kissing, wildly, passionately, in a way they had never really kissed before. In the next minute they were undressing each other impatiently. Iason began biting Riki's throat, causing the mongrel to cry out.

"Oh! That drives me insane when you do that! Hell, yes!"

The Blondie continued his ministrations, at the same time twisting Riki's nipples. Riki arched his back, moaning.

Iason gently hooked a finger in the mongrel's nipple ring, pulling it. "I love that you pierced this for me," he whispered.

"I knew you would," Riki answered. "For the record, it hurt like hell, though."

"You look so sexy, Riki."

Riki toyed with one of Iason's nipples, smiling mischievously. "You'd look hot as hell with your nipple pierced," he hinted.

"Hmmm?"

"You heard me."

"I don't know," Iason hedged.

"Oh, come on. I did it for you."

"I like what you're doing. Suckle me a bit," the Blondie demanded.

"All right, but I hope you'll consider it."

Riki began twisting and sucking Iason's nipples, and the Blondie responded with eager groans and sighs. For some reason, they had never concentrated so much on Iason's nipples, as Riki was the one with this particular erogenous zone. Now Iason was enjoying the attention, unconsciously arching his back in response to the stimulation.

"I want a good taste of you," Riki said provocatively.

"Oh, Riki," Iason breathed. "You mean…?"

"Turn over. Get on your hands and knees."

The mongrel moved to the side as Lord Mink eagerly got into position, his long white-blond hair trailing on the bed. Riki got behind him and spread his ass cheeks apart. "You have the prettiest ass I've ever seen. And no hair. Doesn't it grow down there?"

"Riki," Iason pleaded, turning to look behind him.

"Don't worry, it's coming. Get ready to clutch the sheets."

With that, the mongrel proceeded to lick Iason's backside for all he was worth, swirling his tongue around his sphincter and then up inside the great Blondie, eliciting excited moans and gasps from Lord Mink who, if truth be told, enjoyed this particular kind of stimulation more than about anything.

"Oh, Riki! That's so good," Iason praised. "You're loving me exquisitely!"

The mongrel made no reply, but only worked him with more enthusiasm, wanting to show, with his actions, how much Iason had pleased him.

"Riki, Riki…."

Lord Mink arched his back, offering himself more intimately to his willing partner. Riki took the bait and slithered his tongue in deeper, rimming him wildly.

"I can't take much more," the Blondie warned.

Riki pulled out. "Oh, crap. We don't have any oil!"

Iason only smiled. "Check the drawer on that table next to the bed," he suggested.

The mongrel did, and gasped when he saw the contents. "Toys!"

"What kind?"

"There's this thing," Riki reported, pulling out what looked to be a tube of some kind with a ring encircling it.

"Ah. That's a vibrating pumping sleeve," Iason replied. "Why don't we put it on you? It will lubricate you and slowly pump you while I penetrate you."

"Are you sure?" the mongrel asked, eagerly eyeing the device.

"Of course. I want you to experience as much pleasure tonight as possible."

"How does it work?"

The Blondie helped him put on the device, setting the intensity to low. He didn't want Riki coming too fast.

"Holy fuck!"

"Wait for me, Riki," Iason commanded, searching the contents of the drawer for some oil. When he found a bottle he fumbled with the cork, pouring the contents on his cock with trembling fingers.

"You'd better hurry! This thing is…warm…and wet…and it's…pumping me!"

"I put it on the lowest setting," Iason answered.

"What! You mean it can get even more intense than this?"

"Don't fiddle with the settings. I want us to come together. Lie back."

"Like this?" The mongrel lay back and held his legs back with his arms.

"Perfect."

"Hey! I saw a dildo in the drawer. I'll bet it vibrates. Why don't you put it up your ass while you fuck me," Riki suggested. "That way we both can have some extra fun."

"Can you wait a moment?" the Blondie asked, tempted by the offer, but not wanting Riki to come.

"Yeah, but make it quick. This thing is fucking amazing!"

Iason found the dildo and verified that it did, indeed, vibrate. He lubricated it and put it on a medium setting and then slowly impaled himself on it.

"Oooo. That's sexy as hell," the mongrel remarked.

The Blondie closed his eyes, enjoying the new stimulation. Then he looked at Riki, positioned so invitingly on the bed, holding his legs open and back for him. With something between a growl and a moan, he lubricated his cock and tossed the empty bottle aside. Then he penetrated the mongrel.

For a moment, both of them were too stunned by the physical sensations to speak. It was simply heaven on earth, multiplied by a factor of pi or some other impossibly endless number, taking them both to a whole new place when it came to pleasure.

"Oh, fuck," Riki groaned.

Lord Mink shuddered and thrust again. He was having trouble concentrating, so intense was his pleasure. But fortunately, his body seemed to take control of things, and he began his acquisition, plundering the mongrel for all he was worth.

Riki was almost screaming, his cries were so loud. The combined sensations of his cock being stimulated with the device and Iason fucking him was almost more than he could handle. He knew he was going to come, even though he was trying hard to hold back.

And he knew it was going to be good....

"God yes," he breathed, as the machine pumped his semen from his engorged cock.

Iason was in a similar state of rapture, clenching his teeth as his own seed found release in the familiar terrain of the mongrel's embrace. The vibrating dildo intensified his orgasm beyond belief; he gasped and moaned, and made all manner of interesting sounds.

In short, the Blondie sang.

"Holy shit, that was good," Riki said after a moment.

"Yes," Iason agreed.

"I'm glad. I wanted it to be special. I meant to tell you that I loved you...I was going to tell you that, at the critical moment, but when the moment came all I could do was groan."

"It's enough that you're telling me now," the Blondie answered. "And I love you, too, Riki."

"We gotta keep these toys," Riki declared.

Iason frowned. "Not for every time. Just for special occasions."

"Yeah, okay," the mongrel agreed quickly, and then, after a moment, "Didn't you enjoy it?"

"I did. Very much. I just don't want us to become dependent on toys to pleasure each other."

"Oh, okay. I guess I can see your point."

"We'll keep the toys," Iason decided.

"Iason?"

"Yes?"

"This is one of the best days we've ever had together. I really had...a good time."

"I'm glad, Riki," the Blondie said softly.

A FEW DAYS LATER, IASON WAS IN HIS FAVORITE green chair by the fire in the great hall, where the immense arched windows overlooked the city of Tanagura, distracted by his own thoughts. More specifically, he was thinking about his own new revelations on being a father, and was trying to decide whether he should tell Omaki, and, especially, Yousi, about the matter.

He found that he didn't like the idea of Aranshu being Voshka's pet. Riki had already called him on this, and he knew it was hypocritical, but he couldn't help it—Aranshu was his son, and he wanted better things for him than a life of service in a harem—even in such an influential harem as that which belonged to Commander Voshka Khosi.

He wanted Aranshu with him, here on Amoi—or at least free to choose his own destiny.

And what was Voshka Khosi going to do? This troubled him, as well. After their last conversation, Iason had been expecting some kind of military action from the infamous Commander. But so far, there had been nothing but silence from Alpha Zen.

Iason frowned. Was this good news, or bad news? He really didn't know. He knew he was hardly in a position to make demands about Aranshu, and this bothered him. So rather than relay the information he had discovered about Aranshu's genetic profile to Voshka, he had simply not replied.

As he was sitting there, thinking about these things, almost as if halfway across the Quadrant, the Commander was reading his very thoughts—his communications center lit up with an incoming call.

From Voshka Khosi.

At first, Iason froze. He was almost afraid to answer. Then he got up and hurried over to the communications center, trying to calm himself with another sip of his wine before he sat down and answered the call.

"Iason Mink," he purred.

"So. I wasn't sure if you were going to answer," the Commander said, his lips in a half-smile.

"What can I do for you, Commander?"

"I was wondering if you had anything you wanted to say to me?"

Iason paused for a moment before replying. "In fact, I do have something. In regard to your pet, Aranshu."

Voshka visibly startled at this. It wasn't, of course, what he was expecting. He settled back in his chair. "I'm listening."

"We ran his genetic profile as you requested and, I'm not sure how to tell you this, but we found a match. Several matches, in fact."

"Several? I'm not following you."

"Aristians are capable of having multiple fathers. Aranshu has, in fact, three. All of them Amoian."

"You mean Blondies?"

"Yes."

"But I thought you said Blondies were sterile?"

"That was my belief," Iason replied.

"Interesting. Well, send me the report. I assume you know the identities of the fathers?"

"Yes, I do. Vosh…."

At hearing this old, familiar name, Voshka softened. "Yes?"

"There's something else. I'm not quite sure how to tell you."

"Just tell me. I have no patience for beating around the bush," Voshka replied.

Iason took a deep breath. "In fact, I am one of the fathers," he announced.

Voshka's brow furrowed. "You? I don't understand."

"It's a long story, and not a good one, I'm afraid."

"You said there were three fathers?"

"That is correct."

"Do you know the others?"

"I do."

"Who are they?"

"Omaki Ghan and Yousi Xuuju," Iason answered.

Voshka was silent for a moment. "But...you're all friends."

"Yes."

"I'm not understanding. How is it you're all the fathers of Aranshu?"

"Did Aranshu tell you nothing of his conception?" Iason asked.

"No."

The Blondie sighed. "I'm afraid he won't be pleased when he finds out. You see, the three of us—Omaki, Yousi and I—how shall I put it delicately? When we were young, we once took an Aristian virgin together...that was many years ago. It was a...foolish venture. One that we all regret—that I, at any rate, regret. We had no idea of there being a pregnancy or what even happened to the woman. How is it you found Aranshu, again?"

"On Aristia," Voshka said softly. "He was a gift after an unsanctioned military raid that destroyed his village. I had all the other boys sent back but I kept him—because of his blond hair, actually. I thought he wasn't truly Aristian."

"Ah."

"But I suppose that he was. Half Aristian, at any rate."

"Yes," Iason agreed.

"Do the other fathers know about this?"

"Not yet. I haven't decided whether to tell them," Lord Mink admitted.

"I see."

"In truth, now that I know, I find myself...it's foolish....."

"What? Tell me," Voshka pressed.

"It's just...I'd like to meet him, at least. He is my son."

Voshka fell silent, a look of coldness pressing into his features. "I hope you don't think you're going to take my pet away from me."

"I didn't say that."

"But you're thinking it."

"Vosh..."

Voshka Khosi was finding himself conflicted. He was still angry at Iason, although he had cooled off considerably in the weeks since their last conversation. And he also rather liked Iason Mink—quite a bit, actually. Though he didn't know what to think about the matter regarding his brother, he didn't truly want to be at odds with Iason, or with Amoi.

This new matter regarding Aranshu, however, had thrown him off. Now that he finally had his long-lost pet in his arms again, everything was being threatened by this new information about Aranshu's true heritage.

"I'll be honest. I'm not sure how I feel about your meeting him," the Commander stated.

"I see," Iason said, disappointed.

"Let me think about it."

"Are you going to talk to him about it?"

"I haven't decided."

"Surely he has a right to know," Iason pressed.

"As his Master, I'll decide what's in his best interests," Voshka replied. "That's it for now, Iason."

With that, the Commander abruptly terminated the call, leaving Iason staring at the encrypted Independent Channel frequency logo that had been used for their call. He disconnected from the communications center and then went and sat back down in his chair by the fire, and tried to occupy himself by reading an issue of Tanagura Quarterly.

"Lord Ghan is here," one of the bodyguards announced over the intercom.

"Ah. Send him in," Iason answered.

Omaki entered and looked around expectantly for Aki.

"Come over here, Omaki, I want to talk to you," Iason said. "Yui, get Lord Ghan a drink. What will you take today? A scotch? Some cognac?"

"Cognac sounds perfect," Omaki replied.

Yui hurriedly brought Lord Ghan his cognac, and the two Blondies settled down together by the fire.

"So what is it you wanted to talk to me about?" Omaki asked. "Where's Aki?"

"He's with Sir Elusiax, playing with Suuki. It's a rather delicate subject," Iason began. "I hardly know how to broach the topic."

"Sounds interesting."

"It has to do with…well, with the time you and I and Yousi engaged with that Aristian woman. You, of course, remember?"

Omaki smiled. "I'd hardly forget that. But…after all these years…why are you bringing that up?"

"Well, it turns out that the Aristian conceived. Using the genetic information from all three of us. So, technically, you, and I—and Yousi—are all fathers."

Lord Ghan looked stunned. "What? Fathers? Is this a joke?"

"I assure you, I would not joke about a matter such as this," Iason replied.

"But…that's impossible!"

"Apparently not."

"How do you know this?"

"I know it because our son is Aranshu, Commander Khosi's pet. Vosh had asked me to run his genetic sample against our database as he was convinced Aranshu was a Blondie. It turns out, he was right."

"Our son is Aranshu—that assassin?" Omaki said in disbelief.

Iason nodded. "Yes, that's true. He did assassinate the Aristian royals."

"And now he's…the Commander's pet?"

"Yes."

Omaki shook his head. "I don't know what to say. I never even considered the possibility of being a father."

"Nor I. But, as it turns out, Aranshu is now a grown man, so it's not the same as it would be, if he were a boy."

"That's true. But still…to think that I have a son…I feel all, I don't know…*tingly* inside."

Lord Mink smiled. "I know the feeling."

"Have you told Yousi?"

"No. I don't think he would understand."

"Probably not," Omaki agreed. "It would confuse him."

"Yes."

"Well, I must say, I hardly know what to make of all this. I need to…sit back and think about it."

"I understand completely."

"I'll go visit with Aki now. Thank you, Iason."

"Of course," the great Blondie nodded.

ASKEL, ODI AND AYUDA WERE RELEASED FROM the hospital and so returned to the penthouse, and with them came Toma, Tai and Freyn, who had remained by their sides nearly the entire time during their stay at Tanagura Medical.

Yui was dismissed and returned back to Raoul's suites. And so a sense of normalcy descended over the penthouse, with everyone back—except for Katze, who remained in the hospital, with Daryl at his side.

"ARANSHU," THE COMMANDER said softly.

"Yes?" Aranshu was sitting on the second level of his rooms, enjoying the view of the mountains through the windows. The Commander had spent the night with him in his new rooms, and Aranshu had been especially passionate, wanting to show his appreciation for what Voshka had done for him.

Voshka climbed the spiral staircase and joined Aranshu on the second level, sitting down across from him. "I want to talk to you about something."

Aranshu frowned, wondering what he had done. He couldn't remember having displeased the Commander, but of course, there was always the chance that he had said or done something without realizing he was offending the man.

"What did I do?" he asked.

"Oh, no. You've done nothing. It's…this is a hard question to ask you, so forgive me but, about your mother—did she tell you nothing of your conception?"

Aranshu swallowed hard at the mention of his mother. It was a sore point between them, and for as long as he could remember, the Commander had never been the one to bring up the matter.

He shook his head. "I know nothing of my father."

"I see. Well, then, this may come as something of a shock to you. It turns out that you have a father. Three, in fact."

"Three?" Aranshu repeated, blinking. Although he'd certainly heard of Aristians with multiple fathers, he would never had expected such a situation to be the case for him. He narrowed his eyes. "How is that possible?"

The Commander looked grim. "Your mother was…taken advantage of, I suppose you could say—by three young Amoian Blondies on Amoi."

"You mean they raped her?" Aranshu demanded.

Voshka was quiet for a moment. "I don't know all the details, Aranshu, but it seems like, yes, it was something like that. But you see, that was a long time ago. They've since regretted their actions—or at least, one of them has, and he has expressed a desire to meet you."

Aranshu digested this information, his mind going a thousand directions at once. Part of him wanted nothing to do with men who had raped his mother, but another part—a lonelier part— longed for a connection with some parent.

"They're Blondies?" he repeated, a bit dumbfounded. "From Amoi?"

"Yes. One of them is…quite well known there. Iason Mink, Head of the Syndicate."

"I've heard of him," Aranshu said. "He's my father?"

"One of them," Voshka agreed.

"Who are the others?"

"They are his friends—Omaki Ghan and Yousi Xuuju."

"And they…want to meet me?"

"I don't know about the other two, but yes, Iason wants to meet you," Voshka confirmed. "Do you have any feelings about that?"

Aranshu thought about this for a moment. "I'd like to meet him. And the others, too."

Voshka nodded. "Very well. If it pleases you, perhaps I'll invite Iason and the two others to come and visit us here on Alpha Zen."

"Yes, I would like that," Aranshu said softly. "Commander?"

"Yes, Shu?"

"I would like to be alone for a while."

Voshka nodded. "Of course. I'll leave you to your thoughts."

With that, the Commander left Aranshu's rooms, making for his own bedchamber, where he put in a call to the Mink household.

Voshka Khosi had come to a sort of decision regarding Iason Mink. Perhaps, after all, he'd been too hasty in ending his friendship with the elusive Blondie. There was no absolute evidence that Iason was behind the death of his brother. He had jumped to conclusions in his anger, something that he rarely did, and now he regretted his hasty words.

In truth, when faced with the unhappy prospect of believing that his friend had something to do with Anori's death, the Commander was inclined to accept the more palatable narrative that Lord Mink was a reliable friend, that nothing of the sort had happened, and that their prior friendship could therefore be restored as though nothing had ever come between them. For indeed, it is the case that when confronted with betrayal too great to comprehend, the mind responds by rationalizing that some miscalculation must have been made, seeking to forget transgressions—even very great ones—in an attempt to restore the former order of things.

And so, the great Commander Voshka Khosi, who had been about to destroy the entire planet of Amoi over the murder of his brother, resolved that he had been entirely mistaken on the matter regarding Iason's involvement. He had several reasons for coming to this conclusion. One reason was that he could not imagine that

Lord Mink possessed the deceptive arts that would have been required, considering their sexual history together. Surely his guilt would have prevented him from enjoying sexual congress with the brother of the very man he had murdered. On this point, he was fully convinced, for Iason had been a delightful fuck.

Secondly, during his last conversation with the Blondie, Iason seemed far more preoccupied with Aranshu than with an impending attack from Alpha Zen. Surely, if he had truly been guilty, he would have been shaking in his boots. But the Blondie had seemed cool-headed and rational, not in the least bit concerned that Voshka might be preparing to annihilate his tiny planet.

Thirdly, Voshka simply liked Iason more than he cared to admit. He loved fucking him; the Blondie was a delight in bed. But beyond this, he enjoyed Lord Mink's company—and that, also, of his companions. He hated to see the relationship come to an end.

Fourth, and finally, the Commander simply willed it to not be true that Iason had betrayed him in such a way. It was beyond his comprehension, and so, confronted with such a distasteful, inconvenient fact, he simply chose to ignore it, writing it off as an error in judgment.

It simply could not be true that Iason Mink had killed Anori. And that was that.

As for the Alphazenian ship, and how it had come to be activated on Amoi, he had no answers. It was a troubling fact in his decision to ignore Iason's part in the affair, but once the Commander put his mind to something, he stuck with it. So the ship simply became an irrelevant fact, and oddity that remained unsolved.

The chief advantage of such a decision was that relationships could be restored between Voshka and Iason—and between Alpha Zen and Amoi. And so, as in many cases throughout history, the real truth was buried, ignored, and forgotten, and a new truth was erected in its place, one that was more palatable to all parties involved, and one that did not cause hard feelings or require actions such as accountability or revenge.

And so, with great happiness, Voshka Khosi put in a call to Iason.

"Iason Mink," came the sultry reply with a full visual of the beautiful Blondie.

"Ah, Iason. You do know how to put a smile on my face."

The Blondie smiled in return. "What can I do for you, Vosh?"

"So, you're still calling me Vosh. I like that. It tells me you still think of me as a friend."

"As far as I'm concerned, we've always been friends," Iason replied in a low voice.

"Indeed. And that's how I know you're innocent in this matter. Iason, you must forgive me for my recent call. I was…out of sorts," the Commander said.

"Oh, Vosh. There is nothing to forgive. Friends…sometimes have a falling out. I wasn't really worried."

"Truly?" The Commander seemed surprised at this, given that he had been ready to annihilate Amoi.

"I knew you were angry."

"So everything is as it was, between us?"

"Of course," Iason said quickly, fluttering his lashes.

"Ah, you're flirting with me again. I like that."

"I must protest," Iason said, laughing. "I wasn't flirting."

"No? Then you're naturally sexy, I suppose," the Commander replied with a smile.

"It's good to see you smiling again, Vosh."

"Yes, well. It's not in my nature to be angry." And this was true; Voshka Khosi, though a serious man, was not inclined to fits of rage. Anger was something he did not process well. Indeed, he was, in general, an amiable man who was in a good mood most of the time—although he did have his moments, especially when it came to Aranshu. Thinking of Aranshu reminded him for the reason of his call. "I told Aranshu about you," he stated.

Iason blinked. "What did he say?"

"That he wants to meet you."

"Oh, Vosh. Really?"

"Yes. But I'd like it to be here, on Alpha Zen. So I'm inviting you and the other two fathers to come to Ultanum. Bring Riki. And the whole gang. Come for the summer. What do you say?"

"It sounds delightful. I'll have to…think about it, of course," Iason replied, "but I'll make every effort to come."

"Please do," the Commander said.

AFTER THREE WEEKS OF CAREFUL INTERACTIONS, YUTAKU Iman had finally developed a tenuous rapport with his new pet, Amon. However, he still had not asked the man to perform for him, and Headmaster Sung was beginning to insist that he do so.

Nervously, one day, he made up his mind that he would ask Amon to perform that night. In truth, he was dying to see the man do so. He had already fantasized about it in the privacy of his inner terrain, much to his mortification and shame. He couldn't seem to help it. Amon was such a handsome man—and so very intelligent, two attributes which Yutaku found particularly arousing.

Amon was still in chains—at Headmaster Sung's insistence—though he was allowed the dignity of sitting in a chair. The two of them had formed a little daily routine which involved eating together and discussing some of Amon's readings of the book about the old Qentu Kings Yutaku had given him. Amon was passionate about the book, which Yutaku found endearing. And

Amon, it seemed, was opening up to him, little by little, becoming more and more "comfortable" with him.

While they were having their usual nightly discussion after dessert, Yutaku pushed his chair away from the table, at first only crossing his legs as he watched Amon speak.

Amon eyed him but continued talking as though nothing were out of the ordinary.

Next Yutaku uncrossed his legs, and with a meaningful look at Amon, touched the bulge in his pants.

Amon stopped talking, regarding him curiously.

"There's something we need to discuss, Amon," Yutaku began softly.

A look of anger filled the man's eyes. Although he had been expecting it, he wasn't happy to be confronted with his pet "duties".

"No," he said simply.

"Now, Amon. Be reasonable. I think I've been very patient with you. I want this to be as comfortable for you as possible. But we're simply out of time. Headmaster Sung is demanding that you perform for me, and is shocked that I have yet to elicit a performance from you."

"Sung be hanged," Amon replied. "I won't do it."

"You *will* do it, either one of two ways: willingly, or with me beating you with a whip. I rather detest whips, so I'm hoping you'll choose the route of compliance."

"You don't even have a whip," Amon challenged.

"Oh?" Yutaku pushed back the front of his over-jacket to reveal the whip he was wearing at his waist. "This is top-of-the-line. I got it from Omaki Ghan, who owns the Taming Tower. Trust me, you don't want me to use it on you."

Amon eyed the whip, his resolve seeming to crumble. "Please," he begged.

"No one will see you except me," Yutaku said gently. "Try to…enjoy it, if you can."

"I don't think I can do it."

"Shall we try out the whip?" Yutaku said this with far more confidence than he felt. His heart was beating fast, and he almost felt like giving up on the whole project and running out of the room. But he had come this far, he knew he had to proceed. If he didn't, Headmaster Sung would put *him* under the whip.

Amon looked away, closing his eyes. Then slowly, he rubbed himself in the crotch area.

"Yes," Yutaku whispered. "That's it. Very good, Amon. I'm quite pleased. Now, unbuckle your pants."

Amon slowly fumbled with the buckles as requested but waited to be commanded before presenting himself.

"Show yourself to me," Yutaku directed.

The dark-haired man hesitated.

"Shall I use my whip?" Yutaku asked, placing a gloved hand on his whip holster.

Amon frowned, but obeyed, revealing his immense organ to the watching Blondie.

"Magnificent," Yutaku praised. "Your arousal pleases me. Now, make love to yourself while I watch."

"Please," Amon begged.

"No, no," Yutaku scolded. "None of that. You know you have to do this. It doesn't have to be…a hardship for you. I want you to enjoy it. Go ahead. Close your eyes and think about something—whatever you like. I don't suppose you would consider thinking about me. I'm not such a fool as that. All that's required is that you perform for me, however you can manage it. Would you like some oil?"

"Yes," Amon admitted.

"Ah. Here we go." Yutaku quickly retrieved a vial of oil from his pocket which he had readied before dinner, and tossed it to the man, who caught it with enviable dexterity, his chains jangling. "That's it," he encouraged, when Amon began spreading the oil on his cock.

Amon let his head fall back, his long hair trailing the floor. His legs were wide apart as he began pumping himself, his hand working his cock with familiar ease.

Yutaku caught his breath, watching with unblinking eyes. He unfastened his own pants and impatiently took off his glove with his teeth, stroking himself with eager fingers as Amon masturbated.

He had never been more excited in all his life! Amon Qentu, the notorious Federation rebel, was performing for him, and him alone!

Amon opened his mouth, a small moan escaping his lips. His hand pumped faster, with increasing urgency and obvious skill. This was a man who had pleasured himself many times before, that much was obvious.

Lord Iman eyed Amon's body hungrily—the nipples through his barely-there net top, the hollows at his pelvis, and of course his enormous manhood. He found himself longing for something more: to touch Amon, to drink his seed, or perhaps even to allow the man to do the unthinkable—mount him and fuck him raw.

He shook his head, trying to regain control. He was reaching his ascent and his whole body was shaking. "Oh, Amon," he said, as his glorious captive released his semen in a great spray of pearly white seed that trickled down his hands to the floor. Yutaku was right behind him, ejaculating hard with a fierce groan, and realizing, with the sweet liberation of his own load, that he had finally done it. He had achieved a victory with Amon.

His pet had performed for him.

"Was that Vosh?" Riki asked, when Iason terminated a call on the telecommunications center.

"Yes. He's invited us to come stay at Alpha Zen."

"That's cool. Are we going?"

"I said I'd think about it," Iason answered.

"Why don't we go? I hear their summers are beautiful there."

"They are, indeed."

"So?"

"Would you like that, Riki?"

"Hell, yeah!"

Aki, who had been within earshot of this conversation, piped up with his assessment. "Can I go to Alpha Zen, too, Guardian? Please?"

Iason smiled. "I don't see why not."

Aki cheered, circling the room in a victory march, an Alphazenian toy helmet on his head. "I'm going to see Commander Khosi!"

"Are we really going?" Riki asked.

Lord Mink got up from the terminal. "Yes. I think that would be a splendid idea. It would make Vosh happy, too."

"Yippee!" the mongrel cheered. "So everything is okay between you and Vosh now, right?"

"It appears so."

"You're a lucky bastard," Riki laughed.

"Riki," Iason scolded, frowning.

"I'm just saying. We could have been in a lot of shit if you two hadn't made up."

Lord Mink nodded. "I suppose that's true."

"Damn right it's true. So when can we go?"

"This summer."

"Woo hoo! That's only a few months away!"

"Woo hoo!" Aki said, imitating Riki.

"Can we bring Ios?"

"I suppose I shall have to ask," Iason answered.

"What will we do if we can't take him?"

"I can watch him," Tai offered, who had been listening from the kitchen.

"You'll be coming with us, Tai," Lord Mink said.

"I will?" Tai said with surprise.

"Yes, the entire household will go."

"The entire household?" Toma repeated, from the great hall.

"Yes, Toma. You, as well."

Tai and Toma looked at each other in disbelief. Never in their wildest dreams would they have imagined going on a voyage to Alpha Zen.

"And the bodyguards?" Tai pressed.

"Yes, of course the bodyguards will go," Iason confirmed. "I said the entire household, didn't I?"

"How exciting!" Tai exclaimed.

"What about Ios, then?" Riki asked, frowning.

"I'll ask Vosh about it, next time I call." Iason said.

"Can I bring Suuki?" Aki screamed suddenly.

"Aki, what did I tell you about screaming in the house?" Iason scolded.

"Sorry, Guardian," Aki whispered. "But can I?"

"We'll have to ask Sir Elusiax. If he says yes, then he may go."

"Can I go ask him right now?" Aki asked excitedly.

"You may," Lord Mink answered with a nod.

The precious boy ran from the penthouse, cape flying behind him.

"So what's Ultanum like?" Riki asked.

"From what I've heard, it's changed a lot since I've been there last," Iason answered. "They've built an immense new palace, and lots of other places like museums, landmarks, amusement parks, libraries, stadiums, and the like."

"Amusement parks?" Riki repeated, eyes widening. "Can we go to one?"

"Yes, I suppose," Iason answered, frowning. He wasn't a fan of amusement parks.

"Why are you frowning? It'll be awesome!"

"I don't particularly enjoy rides."

"Why does that not surprise me," Riki said wryly. "But we have to go on the big rides together!"

"If you insist."

"This is going to be a freaking amazing summer!" Riki proclaimed.

Tai and Toma exchanged happy glances, agreeing with this assessment.

AFTER HE WAS PUNISHED BY XANTHUS KAHN, HEADMASTER Sung was forced to take a few days off from the Academy, being not in a state fit to face his students. He felt so guilty about his encounter with Aertis Jin that he issued a reprieve from the usual

Jupiter's Eve lectures with the Blondies—three weeks, to be exact, a declaration that was greeted with exclamations of relief and joy from the Blondies, who despised the lectures and who, with the exception of Iason, had still not memorized their sections of the General Code.

Jupiter's Eve, however, finally came—that is, the Jupiter's Eve marking three weeks since their last session with Konami Sung—and the Blondies reluctantly arrived at the Mink estate for their nightly ritual of dinner, followed by Headmaster Sung's lecture.

And while the dinner was always pleasant enough and something which everyone looked forward to, the second part of the evening was not nearly as happily anticipated as the first, and the Blondies were now in a state of agitation over Lord Sung's now confirmed trysts with the young Aertis Jin, which they nearly all (with the exception, perhaps, of Iason) perceived as putting the Headmaster on tenuous standing as a Disciplinarian.

"I have footage," Xian announced, "that will make your eyeballs fall out."

"I'm sure my footage is equally scandalous," Omaki protested. "I took a good look at it, to be sure."

"I'm sure you did, Omi," Heiku said wryly. "But where did you obtain your footage, Xian?"

"At the Dark Horse, of course," Lord Sami replied. "For whatever reason, old Sung and Jin came to my establishment a few weeks ago and fornicated the night away."

At this, Megala, who was seated in the great hall with the others waiting for the dinner bell to chime, abruptly stood up for no particular reason, rubbing his hands together. "Might I obtain that footage for my collection?"

"Which footage?" Xian asked. "Mine or Omaki's?"

"Yours…that is, both, if possible," Lord Chi answered, looking to Omaki with hopeful eyes.

"That Sung has a lot of nerve lecturing us when he's engaging in salacious affairs," Raoul grumbled. "We ought to confront him about it."

"Goodness, no," Iason protested. "I hope you don't mean to do that in my home this evening?"

"And why not?" Raoul growled. "He'll be at us with that crop whip tonight, make no mistake."

"I must protest," Lord Mink said, frowning. "I'll not have the Headmaster disgraced while I'm the host."

"We might have guessed you'd feel that way, Iason. The Headmaster always did favor you," Raoul said grumpily.

The others all nodded their agreement.

Iason continued to frown. "I'm sure I don't know what you mean."

"Sarius told me an interesting rumor. Apparently a few weeks ago both Sung and Jin were absent from the Academy, and when they returned, both of them were limping," Heiku reported.

Xian shook his head. "What does that mean?"

"It means, most likely, that they felt guilty for their encounters and went to a Disciplinarian to be punished for them," Lord Quiahtenon answered.

"You don't know that for sure," Raoul objected.

"That does sound like something the Headmaster would do," Iason said.

"Well, if we're going to confront him about what he's done, we certainly have the evidence to back it up," Omaki stated. "We probably don't even have to show him the footage—just mention that we have it. Although, for the record, I did bring it with me."

"As did I," Lord Sami said.

"Oh? Might we have a look?" Megala asked with transparent eagerness.

"Certainly not," Iason said, rising to his feet. "Besides, dinner is ready. That was the chime, just now."

"Well, I am hungry," Raoul admitted, rising with a sigh.

"But the footage," Lord Chi said anxiously, looking from Omaki to Xian. "When can I get a look at it?"

Lord Ghan put a hand on Megala's back. "Don't worry, Chi-chi. I brought you a copy to add to your collection. And I hope you brought the blueprints for my seaside estate? The one that's going to be ten times as extravagant as Xian's?"

"Ten times!" Lord Sami exclaimed. "You're delusional!"

"Yes, I brought the blueprints, for both of you," Megala said, following them to the dinner table. He looked at Xian. "Did you bring me a copy of your footage?"

"You can have the copy I brought," Lord Sami answered.

"Oh, wonderful!"

"Sit down, everyone. I have a few announcements to make," Iason said, as he took his seat at the head of the table.

The Blondies, pets and attendants all sat down, including Katze and Daryl, who had joined them specially for that evening.

"How long is this going to take?" Riki demanded, eyeing the roasted pheasant impatiently.

"Riki," Lord Mink sighed.

"What?" the mongrel asked innocently, as though he had no idea why Iason might be upset.

"Must you always make a fuss when I'm trying to make my announcements?"

"Well, must you always make your announcements when we're all ready to eat? I'm starving!"

"Pet!"

Katze nudged Riki, causing the mongrel to wince. "Ow!" he complained. "That hurt!"

"Riki, this is your final warning," Iason said.

Riki opened his mouth and then, realizing that all eyes were on him, thought better of it, and closed it. He looked toward Iason, trying to hide his impatience.

Lord Mink was surprised that the mongrel had quieted without being punished in front of everyone, as usual, and for a moment he lost his train of thought. Then, aware that the entire table was waiting for him to speak, he took a sip of his wine. "I wanted to let you all know that the Commander and I are back on speaking terms."

Everyone sighed their relief, for this had been a matter of some concern to them all.

"That's wonderful news, Iason," Heiku remarked.

"Yes," Lord Sami agreed.

"And as a show of our restored friendship, Vosh has invited me to Alpha Zen for the summer. I've decided that I shall go, and take my entire household with me."

This announcement was greeted with looks of surprise.

"The entire summer?" Raoul asked, looking a little forlorn.

"Yes, and the Commander extended the invitation to any of you who might want to join us. Alpha Zen, as I'm sure you know, has wonderful summers, with delightfully long days and a midnight sun."

The Blondies all chattered eagerly at this.

"I'll go," Raoul said immediately—and no one was surprised. Everyone knew that Raoul wasn't about to spend a summer apart from Iason.

"Very good, Raoul," Lord Mink responded, smiling slightly.

"It sounds like a delightful trip," Heiku said, "but I'm not sure I can take the entire summer off from my work at Tanagura Med."

"Are you certain? Surely someone can cover for you," Iason pressed.

"Well, I'll have to look into it. I would like to go."

"I've always wanted to see Alpha Zen," Xian remarked. "I might just take you up on that invitation, Iason."

"I would be delighted," Iason said, nodding.

"I'll be going, of course," Omaki announced. "Perhaps for the same reason Iason is going: so I can see my son."

The Blondies, with the exception of Iason, all turned to Omaki, puzzled, and blasting him with questions.

"Your son?"

"Whatever do you mean?"

"How much have you drank tonight, Omi?"

"What has Iason got to do with anything?"

Omaki put up a hand, smiling, his eyes twinkling. He looked toward Iason. "Shall I tell them, or will you do the honors?"

Lord Mink, a little flustered that Omaki had mentioned the matter, took a deep breath. "Omaki does have a son on Alpha Zen, in fact. As do I. We're both the fathers of Aranshu, Voshka's pet."

"What!" Raoul bellowed.

"That's impossible," Heiku stated. "Amoian Blondies simply are not capable of having children."

"That's what we thought, of course. But it turns out this belief is incorrect."

Raoul shook his head. "I don't understand, Iason. How can you both be fathers of the same individual—this Aranshu?"

"Aranshu is Aristian," Lord Mink answered, "and Aristian women are capable of conceiving with multiple fathers."

"That's true, actually," Heiku confirmed. "But surely not Blondies? What makes you think so?"

"We ran his genetic signature against Jupiter's database at Voshka's request and it matched up with Omaki and I," Iason explained. "Apparently the Commander already had reason to believe Aranshu might be a Blondie."

"Why would he think that?" Raoul wondered aloud.

"I think it had something to do with the cock-clenching sex," Omaki said, leaning over and putting his hand up as though to hide his answer, which everyone nevertheless heard.

"I don't believe it," Heiku said, crossing his arms on his chest. "You still haven't explained how you both would be fathers of this same individual."

At this, Iason lowered his gaze.

Omaki took the cue, clearing his throat. "There was a…certain incident we both participated in years ago, you see, that involved an Aristian virgin…and well, as it turns out, she conceived after the whole affair."

"I remember that," Xian said quietly.

"I do, too," Raoul said.

"I suppose I do, as well," Heiku sighed.

"And so, I'm a father," Omaki finished.

"As am I," Iason said.

"I'm not a father," Yousi said sadly.

Iason and Omaki exchanged excited glances.

"Oh, but, Yousi, would you *like* to be a father?" Lord Ghan asked.

"Hold on now, I know what you're getting at, but don't confuse him—he won't remember that," Heiku whispered.

"Remember what?" Yousi asked. "And yes, I *would* like to be a father!"

"But Yousi, you already *are* a father!" Omaki said, ignoring Lord Quiahtenon.

"I am?" Yousi said excitedly.

"Yes, you are. You were with us when we took that Aristian virgin years ago."

Yousi sat very still for a moment and then, abruptly, stood up. "I remember that!" he yelled.

"We don't yell in this house," Aki piped up.

"Hush, Aki," Iason said, shaking his head at the nine-year-old.

"I'm sorry," Yousi apologized. "But…I do remember."

"Do you really, Yousi?" Heiku asked.

"Yes, I do! Iason went first!"

Iason reddened at this, recollecting the event. "So I did," he confirmed.

"So I'm a father! I'm a father, too!"

"Yes, you are," Lord Ghan agreed, smiling.

"I want to go to Alpha Zen!" Yousi turned to Heiku. "Can I go?"

"Of course you can go," Lord Quiahtenon assured him.

"You'll go with me, won't you? I want to see my son!"

The physician made up his mind then and there. "Yes. I'll go with you, Yousi. Sit down, now."

Yousi sat back down and drank some water.

"Wonderful," Iason said. "Megala, what about you?"

"I'm afraid I have too much work to do, what with four villas to complete," Lord Chi answered. "But be sure to thank the Commander for the invitation."

"I have a new word for you, Chi-chi," Omaki said. "It's called *delegate*."

"Yes, Megala, you'll be missing out on all the fun," Xian agreed.

"Well," Lord Chi considered, "that is, I also have my…my…er…collections to consider. I'm enjoying viewing them."

"Bring them with you!" Omaki suggested.

"I suppose I could do that," Megala said softly. "That is, if you really think I should go?"

"Of course you should go. We should all go," Lord Ghan proclaimed.

"Are we going to eat?" Riki demanded, his patience, at long last, running out.

"Riki, what did I tell you?" Iason scolded.

"But this is taking bloody forever! And the food is getting cold!"

"The food will stay warm under the warming domes, Riki," Tai said softly.

"Still," the mongrel grumbled. "Are you finished?"

"In fact, I am not," Iason said, giving Riki a warning look, "and you have already earned yourself a spanking, pet."

"For what! I'm just sitting here waiting to eat!"

"Riki!"

"Well, get on with it, then! Sheesh!"

Lord Mink rolled his eyes to the heavens. "Forgive my pet."

"It's all right, Iason," Raoul said reassuringly.

"So, Toma is going to help me with the next part of the announcements. Katze? Could you come here for a moment?"

Toma got up and mysteriously left the great hall.

Katze looked so surprised at being summoned that, at first, it didn't seem like he would respond. Slowly, he got up and made his way to Lord Mink's chair.

"Katze, I know you took a shot for Riki on that unfortunate day at Omaki's villa, and I wanted to thank you for doing that—for trying to save Riki. So this is a small token of my appreciation. Toma?"

Toma came into the hall carrying a beautiful vase.

"Katze, this is a Vergatti. It is worth quite a bit of money. You can sell it if you like, or just enjoy it for what it is. Please take it in appreciation for your noble actions."

"Keep it away from Riki," Raoul advised, and everyone laughed—except, of course, the mongrel.

Katze took the vase, looking visibly touched. "Thank you, Iason."

Lord Mink nodded. "You may return to your seat." The Blondie then presented Ayuda, Odi and Askel all with Vergatti vases and similar speeches, and then, the announcements being finished, the dinner finally commenced, with everyone in high spirits, talking mostly about their upcoming trip to Alpha Zen.

When the Headmaster finally arrived, he was escorted to the table for a bit of dessert—an Aristian Cream-Filled White Cake Smothered in Caramel, while the rest of the Blondies, with the exception of Iason, (having already finished their desserts) looked on, trying their best not to glare at the Headmaster.

"I must, say, Iason, this is the best cake I think I've ever tasted," Lord Sung announced. "Please give my compliments to your chef."

Iason nodded, smiling at Tai, who beamed back his pleasure.

"Gentlemen, I hope you've applied yourselves during these past three weeks and memorized the Code I assigned you," the Headmaster said, sipping his coffee.

The table was dead silent.

"I see. Well, now, with the exception of Yousi—Yousi, you may go home now—shall we adjourn to the great hall now?"

The Blondies all groaned but obligingly made their way to the chairs around the fire, while the attendants helped Tai clear the table and the pets sat or reclined on the floor on the pillows Iason had laid out for them, just as they usually did on Jupiter's Eve.

"I hope you don't mind if I stay," Yousi said to the Headmaster.

"Why would you want to do that?" Lord Sung replied.

"We're having pairings later this evening," the Blondie explained, "and I want to be here for them."

"I see. Very well, then. Join the others, but I shall expect nothing from you."

"Thank you, Sir."

Raoul kept making uninterpretable gestures to Omaki, who shrugged, as though not understanding. Frustrated, Raoul turned to Xian and proceeded to make the same gestures.

Lord Sami shook his head, looking puzzled.

"Raoul, is there something you'd like to say?" the Headmaster finally asked, tapping his crop whip against his leg.

"Er…no." Raoul said, sitting down and glaring at Omaki.

Lord Ghan raised his hands as if in surrender.

"Very well; before we begin, I'll have that logbook. I've given you ample time to produce it, and I think I made it clear what would happen if you did not give it to me today."

Iason reached over to the table next to his chair and retrieved the logbook, holding it up. "Here it is, Headmaster."

Lord Sung looked visibly surprised, taking the book. "Ah. You found it? And where was it, may I ask?"

"It made its way to Alpha Zen via a little stowaway pet," Lord Mink answered. "The Commander contacted us about it and sent it back to us."

"I see. Well, that's settled, then. Now, on to the Code. Who is ready to begin? Raoul?"

Raoul frowned, but stood up. He closed his eyes for a moment, and then began reciting the Code. After he finished two passages, he stopped.

The Headmaster seemed pleased. "Well done, Am. You see what can be accomplished when you apply yourself? I must say, your performance has improved considerably over the last time we met. I hope the rest of your passages will be just as perfectly recited. Proceed."

Raoul cleared his throat before beginning again. "Section IVc."

Everyone waited.

"Section IVc," Raoul repeated, looking a little nervous.

"Yes, Raoul, you stated the section. Proceed." Headmaster Sung tapped his whip against one gloved hand, looking stern.

"The…the…that is, erm, I meant to say: Speed limit in Tanagura. The speed limit in Tanagura is 135 miles per hour. Violators of the speed, with the exception of those with Override Codes, shall be," now Raoul looked at the Headmaster fearfully as he licked his lips, "punished in some form or another, according to—"

"Incorrect," the Headmaster stated. "I shall not give you the correct reading, as you should have mastered it already. Five strikes, Raoul. Turn around."

"Blast it all!"

"Excuse me? Shall we make it seven strikes?"

"But, but, Headmaster," Lord Am pleaded, pointing toward Xian, who looked back in wide-eyed surprise, "first, I think, Xian has something to say to you."

Lord Sung put his hands on his hip, still holding the crop whip. "What's this?" he demanded, looking to Lord Sami.

Xian opened his mouth and then closed it, swallowing hard.

"What is it, Xian? If you have something to say, I suggest you speak up!"

"I…I…that is, actually…."

"Yes?" Lord Sung said, sounding impatient.

Xian looked at Omaki, who shook his head. "Actually, it's Omaki who has something to say."

At this, Omaki pursed his lips together, looking behind him as though not quite hearing.

"Well, whoever has something to say, say it!" Lord Sung roared. He turned to Omaki. "Ghan? You have something on your mind?"

"Me? Ah! Yes, I guess there is the, uh, matter of…of…that is to say, Xian and I have…have…."

"You're exasperating me," the Headmaster announced. "Out with it, whatever it is. What is it you have?"

"What I meant to say is that we have certain…um…footage, you see…of a compromising nature—that is, of a *sexual* nature, of a…a…*devious* sexual nature that, uh, we…wanted to bring to your attention."

The Headmaster stared at him for a moment. "Do you mean to tell me you're confessing to having contraband footage?"

"Well," Omaki began uncertainly.

"Illicit footage of a sexual nature?"

"Yes," Lord Ghan agreed.

"I see. And Xian is confessing to the same thing?"

"I don't know if *confessing* is the right word," Lord Sami said, frowning.

"Of course it's the right word, and do you really think I don't know about your enterprises, the two of you? Of course I know you have salacious footage—I can't begin to imagine what you must possess! I don't know why you felt the need to confess this to me at this moment, but I applaud your doing so. You shall, of course, be punished. Twenty strikes, for the both of you. Anyone else care to make a confession at this time? Raoul? What about you?"

"Pardon me?" Lord Am said, his face turning red.

"You don't want to confess to having had relations with your attendant, Yui?"

"But I was pu-punished for that," Raoul stammered.

"No, you were whipped for having Yui restored. So, you have had relations with Yui, then?"

"Yes," Raoul whispered, bowing his head.

"Twenty strikes for you, also. Anyone else? Megala?"

"I have footage," Lord Chi said softly.

"I see. Twenty strikes, Megala. Anyone else? Heiku?"

"Footage," the Blondie sighed.

"Twenty for you also. Now, who's missing?" The Headmaster walked slowly toward Iason, who kept his head bowed. "Iason? Do you have anything to confess? Hmmm? Do I really have to spell it out for you?"

"I have sexual relations with my pet," Lord Mink said softly.

"Ah. There we are. Twenty strikes, for you as well. Raoul, you're first. Drop your pants and bend over."

"Now, just a minute," Lord Am protested.

"You heard me," Lord Sung hissed. "And don't forget, you have twenty-*five* strikes coming."

"I won't do it. I won't do it, because you're a hypocrite."

"Raoul," Iason said sharply, but the Blondie ignored him.

"What we're trying to tell you is that we have footage of you and Aertis Jin—both at Omaki's villa and then again at the Dark Horse. We can show it to you if you want. I don't see why we should be punished when you're not following the rules."

Headmaster Sung stood very still. After what seemed like an endless moment, he quietly leaned back against one of the hall pillars. "I see," he said. "You've lost all respect for me."

"No, Headmaster," Iason protested.

Lord Sung put up a hand. "No, you're right. I'm completely at fault. I see I can no longer continue these lectures now. I will...consult with Xanthus Kahn, and see if he can take over for me. But as for now, gentlemen, consider this evening's lecture to be at an end."

The Blondies all frowned as the Headmaster made his way out of the penthouse. The man seemed broken and sad. This was not what any of them wanted...and now it was too late.

As soon as Konami departed, the Blondies began arguing.

"I told you not to disgrace him in my home, Raoul," Iason said, obviously very unhappy with the outcome.

Raoul frowned. "I didn't know he would be like *that*."

"Did you see his face?" Heiku murmured. "It was like we *killed* him."

"Well, to be fair, he *was* fucking Jin," Omaki pointed out.

"I'd rather face Konami than Xanthus Kahn," Xian said, shivering. "I still have nightmares about him and that whip."

Raoul nodded. "We all feel that way."

"What can we do now? It's too late to take it back," Megala said.

"It's never too late to say you're sorry," Yousi said simply.

The Blondies were quiet for a moment, considering the wisdom of Yousi's advice.

"We could bake him a cake," Heiku suggested.

"He does love cake," Omaki nodded.

"Right. And all of us go over there to his place and apologize, and ask him to continue with the lectures, rather than Xanthus Kahn," Xian said.

"We don't have time to bake a cake," Iason said. "We'll just buy one."

"Excuse me, Master Iason?" Tai said uncertainly, not wanting to intrude on the conversation, but feeling, when it came to cakes, he had some important information.

"Yes?" Lord Mink asked, turning to him.

"I have a Triple Aristian Chocolate Cake already baked. I was going to serve it tomorrow."

"Perfect," Iason said. "Thank you, Tai."

"That settles it. Let's get it boxed up and take it over to him now," Heiku said.

The Blondies all nodded their agreement.

SO, LEAVING THEIR PETS AND ATTENDANTS BEHIND, the Blondies boxed up the cake and put a bow on it and then crowded into a few vehicles and made for Konami Sung's estate.

When they arrived, they were relieved to see Lord Sung's vehicle already there. They went to the door and were met by the Headmaster's attendant, who looked surprised to see a group of Blondies standing outside his door.

"Just a moment," he said.

Konami Sung came to the door, looking equally surprised.

"Headmaster, we came to apologize," Iason began.

"We brought you a present," Raoul said, handing him the boxed cake.

"Goodness," the Headmaster said, taking the gift. "What on earth? I can't imagine what this might be."

"It's a cake," Yousi announced.

"Yousi," the Blondies all groaned.

"I'm sorry," Yousi said, frowning.

"It's quite all right, Yousi," Konami reassured him. "I happen to love cake."

"We know you do," Omaki said.

"About today, we don't want you to think we've lost respect for you," Heiku said.

Xian nodded. "We want you to continue with the lectures, just like before."

"We all have our weaknesses," Iason said softly. "We don't think less of you for it."

"Well now," Konami said, his eyes watering slightly, "isn't that nice. I certainly wasn't expecting this."

"So will you come back, like before?" Raoul asked.

"Yes, of course. Thank you, gentlemen, for the cake. I'll bid you goodnight now."

"Goodnight Headmaster," the Blondies all said in unison.

"There now," Heiku said, once they made their way back to their vehicles. "That worked out quite well, I think."

"Look at the stars," Yousi said, gazing up at the sky.

"Yes, they're beautiful," Heiku agreed.

"Wait a moment," Omaki said, as Iason started to get into his vehicle.

"What is it?" Iason asked.

"This is nice, all of us together, right now," Omaki continued. "Let's just enjoy it for a moment. Life is so…fleeting and fragile. You never know when it'll all be gone."

The Blondies stood together for a moment, contemplating this.

"We have to get back to the penthouse," Iason remarked. "They've probably turned the place upside-down by now. And I owe Riki a spanking."

"You still haven't got him tamed yet, have you, Iason?" Heiku observed.

Lord Mink only rolled his eyes to the heavens. "Some things never end."

"Well, he did a good thing for you at the Public Whippings," Raoul said thoughtfully.

"Yes, he did," Iason agreed, smiling. "That counts for something."

"It does, indeed. We have a pairing tonight, don't we?" Raoul suddenly remembered.

"Two pairings," Megala confirmed.

Xian put a hand on Omaki's shoulder. "It was a nice thought. But I don't know what you're going on about. We'll always be together."

"Yes," Yousi said merrily, "some things never end."

# Chapter 4-
# Raoul's Party

MEGALA CHI, FOR ALL HIS DEVIOUSNESS, WAS a brilliant architect. He made good his promise to Raoul Am to finish his villa in three weeks, to make up for the alleged "grievance" that had been done to Lord Am when the Blondie was in a compromised state—a grievance that, though not *formally* admitted to, was nevertheless supposed by everyone to be true given that Lord Chi hired hundreds of builders in a desperate attempt to meet the imposed deadline of finishing the villa.

And finish it, he did. It was a masterpiece of architecture, a wonder to behold, with twelve fountains in a series of formal gardens that had been designed by none other than the legendary Blondie Katan Zavi, who sculpted Iason Mink's gardens and, it was said, even journeyed to Alpha Zen to plan the gardens of Commander Voshka Khosi.

Lord Am, also true to his word, sent out formal invitations to a party to be held at his new seaside villa, including in his guest list Yutaku Iman, Katan Zavi, Kobin Nu, Norju Faire, Elusiax Kain, Sanyara Ven, and, oddly, Xanthus Kahn, Headmaster Konami Sung, and Aertis Jin, in addition to the expected picks—Iason Mink, Omaki Ghan, Xian Sami, Megala Chi, Heiku Quiahtenon, and Yousi Xuuju (the rest of the "Rebel Six", plus Yousi, to be exact), along with their households.

Everyone accepted, though Yutaku Iman replied that his pet was still in chains and could not come, which was exactly what was expected. The memory of the encounter with Amon was still too fresh in everyone's minds, and it would have been awkward, were Iason or Riki to confront Amon, even in his humiliated state of newly achieved pethood.

The day of the party arrived and Riki, in a bad mood about having to wear chains, was moping on the balcony. Iason found him there, smoking.

"As much as you smoke, we'll have to replace your lungs with bionic ones," the Blondie said.

"That'd be cool," Riki answered.

"Riki," Iason sighed.

"Well, it would. And I still want a bionic arm."

"I don't want any of your body parts replaced by synthetic units. I want you whole and complete, just as you are."

"Part of me is already missing. I got my nipple pierced, remember?" the mongrel said saucily.

"Piercing is excluded," the Blondie replied with a smile.

"Well, I hope you don't want me to pierce anything else, because that nipple piercing hurt like hell."

"If I want you to be pierced, you'll be pierced," Iason stated matter-of-factly.

"You're one sick, sadistic fuck, you know that?" Riki said, exhaling directly in Iason's face.

"Riki! How many times must I tell you *not* to blow smoke in my face!"

"Well, you could see I was out here smoking, why did you come out?"

"Because I want to talk to you about tonight."

The mongrel rolled his eyes. "Here we go."

"Riki, I expect you to be on your best behavior tonight. Especially considering it's Raoul's new home and his party, I don't want anything ruined by one of your little tantrums."

"Raoul and I get along now. Haven't you gotten the memo?"

"All the same, can I trust you to be on your best behavior?"

"Yes," Riki answered with an exaggerated sigh.

"Good."

"Do I really have to wear my chains?"

Iason looked away. "Not even open for discussion, pet."

"But some of the other pets don't wear chains! Why must I?"

"Riki! What did I just tell you?"

"Just answer me!" the mongrel insisted.

Iason sighed, turning to face him. "Because it pleases me. Because…I wish it so. Riki, there will be a number of guests there tonight we don't usually see. We need to arrive in the proper fashion."

Riki knew that he was getting nowhere, and that he was risking annoying his Master in the process. He resigned himself to wearing the chains, deciding that, to make up for it, he would deliberately make them late for the party. That way, most of the pets and attendants wouldn't see him arrive and would already be off in their designated party area. "Whatever. How many drinks can I have?"

"Three."

Although Riki was tempted to protest, three was better than *two*—which is what Iason usually said—so he opted not to say anything.

"Try not to use vulgar language tonight, Riki. There will be some very distinguished Blondies there. I'm sure their pets will report anything they hear you say."

"Geez, anything else? I don't suppose you'd consider removing my ring restrictions?"

"Absolutely not."

"But Katze said there are going to be holo-projections for the pets and attendants. I'll be in agony!"

"I want you to save it up for later tonight," the Blondie replied, looking meaningfully at him.

"I'm always ready for you."

The Blondie tipped Riki's chin up toward him with two gloved fingers. "I want you so excited tonight, you're quivering for me."

"Are you bringing toys?"

"I'm being serious."

"So am I."

"Put that cigarette out. I want to kiss you." Iason moved his hands to Riki's waist, pulling him close.

The mongrel threw the cigarette over his shoulder, and it went spiraling down in red streaks to the city below.

"Riki! How many times must I tell you—"

"Yeah, yeah. What about that kiss?" Riki asked, his eyes gleaming in the moonlight.

The Blondie kissed him, softly, and then broke away. "Must you vex me?"

"Kiss me again."

"I'm already aroused."

"So? We can do it before we go."

Iason looked at his watch. "No. We haven't time. Come, let's get your chains on."

"Boy, you sure do know how to ruin a moment," Riki complained. "Anyway, I have to change first."

"We haven't time for that, Riki."

"But I can't wear this!"

"Why not? You look perfectly fine."

"I had a special outfit planned. Please?"

Lord Mink looked vexed with the delay, but nodded. "Very well. But *hurry*, Riki."

Iason and Riki finally arrived at the party, along with Tai, Toma, Ayuda, Odi, Askel, Freyn, and one of the new bodyguards, Zanus, and were greeted personally by Raoul Am, once they were announced.

"Welcome, Iason! You look fabulous tonight. Riki." The Blondie nodded in the mongrel's direction to acknowledge his presence.

Riki nodded back.

The old animosity between the two of them had faded away, ever since Raoul had witnessed what Riki had done for Iason at the Public Whippings. Although he would never *verbally* admit it to anyone, the Blondie actually respected the mongrel for what he had done that day—as evidenced by his painting of Riki, which was all the talk in Tanagura. His feelings for Lord Mink, however, remained unchanged, and that was perhaps still a sore point between them.

Tonight, however, he was all smiles.

"Come in, all of you. Get some punch and cake. Everyone is already here."

"Forgive our lateness," Iason purred. Although he seemed calm about it at the moment, earlier, at the penthouse, he had been in a rage when Riki had delayed their leaving, pretending that he was having trouble dressing, or finding his boots, or—to top it off—locating his cigarettes. Iason had threatened to confiscate the smokes as punishment for Riki making them late, but the mongrel had begged and pleaded with him not to take them away, and the

Blondie had finally acquiesced, not wanting to get the night off to a bad start.

"Nothing to forgive, although the party couldn't really start without *you*," Raoul replied.

Iason looked around. "My. This is fabulous, Raoul."

The seaside villa had an enormous foyer with a ceiling that went to the heavens, graced with a chandelier.

"You haven't seen anything," Raoul said proudly. "Come, come!"

They followed the great Blondie inside the villa, marveling at the luxurious architecture—the hall columns and immense, spacious rooms with arching windows and doors. When they got to the great hall, they stopped, stunned.

The hall was simply breathtaking. It was lined with twelve grand columns that went down the center of the hall, all in aquamarine marble—much like Iason's penthouse. There were statues and paintings all the way down the hall, and fountains coming out of the walls. The hall was furnished with grand Aristian Royal imports, the settees, sofas, and chairs all trimmed with gold and stunning down to the last detail. The chair feet terminated in the shape of Icarian lion's paws, for instance, and the plush fabric was in elegant pink, gold, and light green. The hall boasted another chandelier—this one even bigger—and the walls were lined with mirrors as well as fantastic paintings all made by Raoul.

One, painting, in particular, caught Riki's eye. It was in the very center of the hall, flanked by two statues, as if on display. The painting depicted Riki, on the day of the Whippings, standing in front of Iason to prevent Xanthus Kahn from striking him again!

"You really *did* paint me," Riki said in disbelief, stopping in front of the painting.

"I did," Lord Am agreed. "I happen to think it's one of my best."

"Oh, Raoul," Iason said. "It's stunning. Everything—the painting, the villa—it's…astonishing, really."

"It is, isn't it?" Raoul agreed happily.

"Ah, Iason's here. The party can officially begin," Omaki announced from one of the chairs.

Everyone turned and greeted the Blondie with cheers and toasts.

There was music playing in the hall, but unlike Omaki's parties, which boasted erotic, heart-stopping dubstep beats, Raoul offered a more refined approach—a small orchestra was playing Icarian classical music in one corner of the hall.

Riki waited impatiently to be let out of his chains, hating the ritual and anxious to be off with the other pets and attendants. Tai, Toma, and the bodyguards had already made their way to the party room.

"You've brought Riki—but where's his spanking machine?" Xian asked, and the Blondies all laughed.

The mongrel frowned.

"He's on good behavior today, for the *most* part," Lord Mink replied, unfastening Riki's chains.

"Well, that's a first, isn't it?" Heiku quipped, and everyone laughed again.

Iason leaned down and whispered in Riki's ear. "Never mind them. You go and have a good time tonight. And you may have *four* drinks."

Smiling, Riki sauntered away, hands in pockets, from the Blondies in the direction Raoul indicated he would find the pets and attendants, glad to be free of his hated chains, and thrilled that Iason had given him additional drinking permissions, especially after he had made them late to the party.

"Speaking of Riki, I say tonight we see him pair," Omaki piped up.

"Hear, hear," Xian said, raising his glass as if in toast.

The others there similarly raised their glasses, toasting the idea. "Hear, hear!"

Iason frowned at this, looking decidedly unhappy with the idea.

"Now, now, let him get settled in," Raoul said, coming to Iason's rescue.

"Iason, is it true you've never shown your pet?" Kobin Nu asked.

"I'm afraid it is," Headmaster Sung answered for him.

"Jupiter can't be pleased with that," Norju Faire remarked.

"No, indeed," Xanthus Kahn agreed.

"You know the only reason she tolerates it is because it's *you*, Iason," Sanyara Ven stated. "You'd do well to show Riki and appease her, especially after…."

Although Sanyara didn't finish his thought, everyone knew where he was going with it.

*Especially after the Public Whippings.*

Lord Mink, finding his way to an empty seat and sitting down gracefully, said nothing, but his expression answered them well enough.

"Come now, let's not spoil the party by ganging up on Iason," Raoul said. "I'm willing to show Regiland tonight."

"We've seen Regiland," Megala offered unhelpfully.

"Yes, we've *just* seen him, in fact," Xian agreed. "I vote for a new pairing."

"Let's change the subject," Raoul insisted, when he saw Iason's look.

Meanwhile, Riki had found the party room for the attendants and pets and was surprised to see so many girls there. He did a double-take when he recognized the females he had insulted at Cornucopia back in Midas—Emerald and Elisif—in a group with some other girls that included Ima. He saw there, too, Jewel—the girl who had once demanded an apology and who was the *real* reason he had run away from Iason.

The bodyguards were all sitting at one table, hunched together and looking at some device, seeming serious, as though they were on duty.

Katze waved him over to a table where he and Daryl were sitting. Riki walked over, glad to see them both.

"Isn't this great?" Katze asked.

"Hmmm? Oh, yeah. I guess. Did you see my painting? The one Raoul did of me?"

"I saw it. Everyone saw it."

The room had a huge holo-projection going on that played pairings, and there were strobe lights in various colors. Large cylindrical tubes full of dripping orange, purple and red liquids went from the ceiling to the floor, and there was a live band playing modern Midas street music.

"Sit down. I have something for you," Katze said, grinning.

"What is it?" Riki wondered.

Katze held up a small device, smiling. "It's an illegal import. A D64-Reverse Modulator. It scrambles the codes on D-type rings and releases them temporarily. I'll release your ring for tonight— but you owe me."

Riki's eyes opened wide. "Are you for real?!"

"Yep. I just need to…get a little close. Don't think this is a come-on or anything," Katze said, as he brought the device near Riki's groin area.

"I can feel something…hey! You did it!" Riki exclaimed.

The device, as if confirming the success, made a happy little beep.

"Told you. You're good to go for about 24 hours. Then it will wear off as the D-ring security figures out it has been compromised and re-scrambles the code. Fortunately, D-rings aren't too sophisticated—at least in *my* opinion."

"Katze you're the greatest! I wasn't even looking forward to tonight, but now I can enjoy myself!"

"Yeah, I figured it would be torture for you otherwise. What with all the girls and the holo-projection going on."

"Oh, I don't think much of the girls," Riki said quickly.

"No?"

"They seem perched too high for my taste."

"That they are. The hot blond there is Emerald, Norju Faire's pet, and the brunette is Elisif, the pet of Headmaster Sung. And that girl to the left that they're talking to is Jewel, the pet of Kobin Nu."

"Yeah, I know. We've met."

"You have? *All* of them?"

The mongrel shrugged. "It didn't go so well."

"Well, the one with the brown hair is Shima, Sanyara Ven's pet. Have you met her?"

"No. She's not my type, though."

"Well, there's Ima. But I guess you should stay away from *her*."

"Yeah," Riki said, a little sadly.

Katze blinked. "Is there something going on I don't know about?"

"Well...Ima miscarried the baby. It was mine."

"Seriously?" Katze looked toward Ima. "I thought she looked pretty thin to be carrying."

"Yeah. Iason was going to let me keep it, too."

"No shit?"

"I'm sorry, Riki," Daryl said softly.

"Thanks."

"Yeah," Katze agreed, nodding his head. "I'm sorry, too."

"Well, what's done is done," Riki said, not knowing that he was repeating Iason's very words to Heiku. "Anyway, Iason is building an Orphanage for me in Midas. *And* he got me a puppy!"

"For real?" Katze put a cigarette in his mouth and then nodded toward Riki. "Hey, can I bum one of your fancy cigarettes?"

"Sure." Riki pulled out his pack of Dark Baccalias and handed Katze a smoke.

"An Orphanage, huh? Bet that's costing him a fortune."

"What's your puppy's name?" Daryl asked.

"Ios," Riki answered.

"Like the moons, or like the lovers?" Daryl wondered.

Riki shrugged. "Both, I guess."

At that moment Ru and Kahlan came over and sat down with them. "Are we interrupting?" Ru asked.

"No, no. Please join us," Katze said. "I hope you don't mind if we smoke."

"Mmmm, Dark Baccalias," Kahlan said longingly.

"Want one?" Riki asked, pushing the pack toward him. "Take one, if you like."

"Seriously?"

"Hell, yeah."

Yui came over with a tray of hors d'oeuvres. "Would you all like something to eat?" he asked.

"Definitely," Riki answered, taking a generous portion of the appetizers for himself.

"Save some for the rest of us," Katze laughed.

"Oh, there's plenty in the back," Yui reassured him.

"Do you need help serving, Yui?" Ru asked.

"If you don't mind," Yui replied. "I haven't offered anything to the girls yet."

"I'll help you," Ru offered, getting up.

"Thanks."

Sarius came over to their table, sitting down without being invited. "What are we talking about?"

"Some really *juicy* gossip," Riki answered.

"Oh, really? Do tell," Sarius said with a grin.

"See those girls over there? Emerald, Jewel and Elisif? Well, I heard they had a threesome the other night—totally unsanctioned, of course—and when their Masters find out, they're really going to be in for it."

Sarius listened with wide eyes, eagerly digesting this unbelievable piece of information, not for a moment doubting its veracity. He quickly excused himself, anxious to pass this rumor along.

Katze nudged Riki in the ribs with his elbow. "Idiot. You'll really get it when they find out who started that rumor."

"Ouch," the mongrel complained, holding his side as though in terrible pain.

Just then Toma and Tai joined the group, along with Megala Chi's attendant Nomi and his pet Shimera, Xian Sami's attendant, Juthian, and Omaki's pet Enyu.

"Hey cat-boy," Riki said, eyeing Enyu suspiciously. "Are you rutting now?"

"As it happens, I am *not* in my interval," Enyu replied.

"Thank heavens for that."

"I don't remember you objecting before," the Xeronian remarked.

Riki darkened but said nothing.

"Is anyone watching this?" Katze nodded toward the holo-projection. "It's hot as hell."

Everyone turned their attention to the flic, which depicted two young males enjoying sex together.

"Fuck, yeah," Riki said, unzipping his pants.

"Riki!" Shimera admonished. "You're not planning to climax in front of us all, are you?"

"Why not?"

"Well *I* don't care to watch."

"Then don't."

"Anyway, don't you have restrictions on your D-ring?"

The mongrel only grinned, taking out his cock and starting to pleasure himself.

Shimera shielded his eyes as if offended.

"Hey," Sarius said, coming back from the great hall, "you should hear what they're talking about in there."

"What is it?" Tai asked.

"They're talking about a pairing."

"Oh really? With who?" Katze wondered.

"That's what's so interesting," Sarius said, grinning.

"Oh, God," Riki groaned.

"Well, who is it?" Toma asked impatiently.

"It's...Riki and Ima."

Just then the mongrel came, with a look of shock and surprise on his face.

"Whhhaaaat?" he asked slowly.

Sarius nodded. "At first Iason said *no*. But the Blondies kept pressing him until he finally agreed. My Master wasn't too keen on the idea, either. But the Headmaster talked him into it."

"You mean we're really going to pair? In front of everyone? *Now*?"

"Yep. Your Master should be coming for you any moment."

"But I just came!"

"That's your problem."

Lord Mink, was indeed, coming toward the table—and Lord Quiahtenon was heading toward Ima.

Riki stealthily zipped up his pants, wiping his hand on the underside of the table.

"Riki, get up. I need to talk to you."

"Huh?" Riki said, standing up slowly.

"I need you to…perform for me tonight. With Ima."

"You mean *pair* with her?" Riki asked incredulously.

"Yes."

The mongrel shook his head. "I don't believe it."

"Come, the others are waiting." Lord Mink refused to look at him.

"But…."

"Riki! Obey me at once!"

"Okay, okay! Sheesh!" The mongrel raised his hands in surrender, following Iason out of the room and up to the great hall, where all the Blondies whistled and made a clamor at his entrance.

"Riki!" they cheered, raising their punch glasses to salute him.

Riki frowned, looking toward Iason, but the Blondie had retreated to his seat, his head down.

"Ima!" the Blondies cheered next, when Ima entered the room. Heiku looked just as displeased as Iason, and grumpily made his way to a chair to sit down.

Riki and Ima stared at each other.

"Fuck," Riki whispered.

"That's what you're supposed to *do*, not say," Xian quipped. The other Blondies laughed.

The mongrel looked questioningly back at Iason, but the Blondie refused to return his gaze. Riki looked again at Ima and realized, for all her hotness, he was *not* in a state to fuck her.

He was not the least bit aroused, having just come.

"Kiss her," Omaki suggested.

Ima blinked her long lashes at him and Riki swallowed. Normally this would have made him go rigid in an instant, but tonight was a different story. He made a clumsy attempt to kiss her, but pulled away, frowning.

"I think we have a problem," Xian noted quietly.

Some of the other Blondies nodded.

At that point, Iason finally looked up and, upon apprehending that Riki was not the least bit aroused, looked profoundly relieved.

"It happens," Kobin Nu said.

The mongrel reddened, hanging his head.

Ima put a hand on her hip, looking offended.

"Perhaps he's not attracted to her," Omaki suggested innocently, much to Iason's delight.

"My Golarian would love a female like that," Xanthus remarked.

"Go get him. We're not going to see anything from Riki today," the Headmaster sighed.

Riki stood for a moment, unsure whether he was allowed to leave. When he looked over and saw Iason's smile, he knew that things had worked out, miraculously, in his favor.

"Come here, pet," Iason said softly.

Riki dutifully trotted over to his chair and knelt down to hear what his Master had to say.

"You don't need to be ashamed," Lord Mink whispered. "It's not your fault that you couldn't get an erection. Now, go back to the others and enjoy the rest of your evening."

The mongrel nodded, backing away. He couldn't believe he was getting away with jacking off! Iason didn't even suspect he had tampered with his D-ring! And he was actually *happy* that he couldn't perform! Things were working out perfectly. Now maybe Iason wouldn't be so jealous of Ima.

Ima glared at him as he left and he slinked away, feeling a little embarrassed. But, after all, he *had* just come minutes before. It was too much to expect him to perform again so soon.

When Riki re-joined the group, they looked at him in surprise.

"Back already?" Katze asked.

The mongrel shrugged. "I couldn't do it."

"What do you mean you couldn't do it, Riki?" Enyu asked.

"I mean, I couldn't get it up for her. So they're asking for Golarian now."

"Well, you *did* just come," Daryl said softly.

"Yeah."

Shimera seemed greatly amused by this, snorting. "He couldn't get it up! Ha ha ha!"

"Shut up or I'll come over there and shove your dick up your ass!"

"You can't talk to me that way!" Shimera said, frowning.

"Go ahead, run and tell your Master," Riki said. "You're pathetic."

"Well! I *will* tell my Master!"

"Riki," Katze said in a low voice. "Cut it out. You know he *will* tell Lord Chi, and then Iason will come looking for you."

"I don't care if he does."

"Hmmmph! You're just lucky I don't feel like getting up at the moment," Shimera said, turning up his nose.

In fact, Shimera knew *he* would be in trouble if he ran to his Master and complained about Riki, because Lord Chi had chided him for his behavior at Omaki's bash and had specifically warned him not to get into a fight with the mongrel.

Riki laughed. "Whatever." Then he looked at Katze. "Hey! We never had that crunching contest!"

"You're still going to hold me to that, after I've been shot?" Katze retorted.

"You just know you'll lose. I'll give you an advantage—I'll start doing twenty before you start."

Katze frowned. "I don't need an advantage. I can still whip your ass."

Daryl shook his head. "Don't do it, Katze."

The auburn-haired youth smiled back at him. "I'll be fine."

"Let's do it, then! Right here!"

"Woo hoo, a contest!" Sarius announced.

"What's the prize?" Shima asked, as she and the other girls came over to see what was going on.

"Loser has to give Iason Mink a massage," Toma reported, having remembered the contest from before.

"That doesn't sound so bad," she replied, looking confused.

"Well, it was originally, loser has to give the *winner* a massage, but Iason changed the prize," Riki explained.

"Oh, I see."

"Where should we do this?" Katze asked, standing up.

"How about on this raised platform?" Sarius suggested, pointing to one of the many platforms of different heights that graced the room. "That way we can all see."

The contestants got up on the platform and laid down on it, assuming the starting position.

"Who is going to count me?" Riki asked.

"I will," Tai volunteered.

"I'll count Katze," Daryl said.

Sarius stood up on the platform, assuming the role of the contest manager. "Then…on your marks, get set, go!"

Riki and Katze both started doing their crunches. Though both of them were extremely fit, from the very start it was clear that Katze was having trouble.

"Don't do this," Daryl said between counts. "Stop if you need to. I don't mind if you lose."

Riki, who was ahead of Katze on the count, considered the fact that the eunuch had taken a bullet for him. He suddenly realized he didn't want Katze to lose—not if he was struggling because he was in pain. Katze deserved better than that. Besides…he owed him for the D64-Reverse Modulator.

Riki groaned loudly, pretending to have trouble finishing a crunch.

Katze, encouraged by this, pushed himself to do a few more.

The mongrel made a fuss, panting, and then collapsed back.

Katze, grinning, finished his count one ahead of Riki's, and so won the competition.

"I knew I could beat you. You're getting out of shape, Riki," the eunuch gloated.

"Yeah, whatever." Riki smiled to himself, knowing that he had let Katze win.

"Katze is the victor! Riki has to give Iason a massage!" Sarius proclaimed.

"Hmmm." Shima said, eyeing Riki's perfectly formed six-pack suspiciously.

The mongrel caught her eye and winked at her.

Shima blushed and turned away, giggling with the other girls.

"I thought you said she wasn't your type," Katze remarked.

"I guess she grew on me," Riki answered.

"Ima isn't going to like it, if you're flirting with another girl."

"Well, Ima isn't too happy with me right now anyway."

"Hmmm."

Suddenly Riki turned his head. "What's that sound?"

"Can you be more specific? There's a lot of noise going on."

"It sounds like...can it be?" Riki started up the stairs that led to where the Blondies were converged in the great hall.

"Hey! Where are you going, Riki?" Katze demanded.

"Shhhh!"

Riki passed Golarian and Ima as he made his way up the stairs. Golarian smirked at him. Riki frowned, saying nothing. He kept climbing the stairs, and as he moved away from the pet and attendant party room, the sound became more clear. It was music. More specifically, it was the sound of someone singing.

A beautiful, deep, rich voice.

Riki got to the top of the stairs and peeked his head around the corner into the great hall. There he saw Iason standing. Iason was singing!

*Before I knew what stars were*

*You showed me how to fly*

*I never knew the way to go*

*Until you took me high*

*Above the moon, where I learned the way*

*To chase the shadows of the day*

*And still I wonder why*

*My heart beats so when you are near*

*Why darkness comes when you're not here*

Riki could see Raoul watching Iason with absolute adoration in his eyes. He frowned, backing away.

In that moment Riki knew, with absolute certainty, by the way his heart felt, that he was in love with Iason Mink. This was not a new revelation, by any means, but he could feel his heart pounding with that certainty.

And Raoul loved Iason, too. That much was obvious.

It was funny. In all the time he'd been with Iason, he'd never once heard him sing.

AFTER THE BLONDIES ENJOYED AN ENTHUSIASTIC, ALBEIT quick, pairing between Golarian and Ima, Iason was asked to sing.

Iason tolerated the ribbing over Riki's being unable to perform, privately pleased with the mongrel's impotency. He knew perfectly well that Riki was able to perform—at least in the privacy of his penthouse. He wasn't looking to impress anyone. He was especially thrilled over the fact that Riki had been unable to become aroused over Ima, the very pet Iason had been so jealous of for so long. The episode had put to rest a major brooding point for the Blondie, allowing him to truly relax and enjoy the party.

Though he normally would have refused the request, tonight he decided to humor Raoul and sing for once, which, he could tell, made the Blondie very happy.

Once Iason finished his song, everyone applauded, and the great lord sat down.

"Magnificent," Raoul praised, especially loudly.

"That was absolutely divine, Iason," Lord Sung agreed, nodding.

"I've just thought of a game," Heiku proclaimed, suddenly.

The Blondies all groaned.

"We hate your games," Xian proclaimed.

"I'll pretend I didn't hear that. Anyway, you'll love this game. It's called Spank the Pets. What are you doing over there by the punch bowl, Omi? Come over here so you can hear this."

"I'm getting punch," Omaki said defensively.

"You've been standing there for a long time. You missed Iason's song!"

"I heard it. Does anyone want punch, while I'm here?"

"I do," Xian said.

"I'll have some as well," Megala said softly.

Katan, Kobin, Norju, Elusiax, Sanyara, Xanthus, Headmaster Sung, Aertis and Yutaku all raised their glasses.

"Everyone wants punch," Raoul announced. "But let Yui get it. Yui!"

Yui was immediately at his side, looking breathless.

"Bring everyone more punch."

"I don't care for any more," Iason replied.

"Oh, you *must* have more," Omaki insisted.

"I was drinking wine."

"But the punch is delicious!" Lord Ghan exclaimed, making a toast in the air. "To Raoul's punch!"

"We don't have our cups yet," Megala said.

"Omi, you're ruining the explanation of my game," Heiku grumbled.

"How does the game go?" Kobin asked politely.

Heiku smiled. "Ah. It's very simple. We all gather our pets, and we spank them. Whoever's pet can last the longest, wins!"

"What do you mean by *last the longest?*" Xian demanded. "We can just go on spanking them forever!"

"No no no, there's the catch. They can't make any noise. If they cry, or make a sound, they're out of the game."

"My Emerald won't last long," Lord Faire remarked, and the Blondies all laughed.

"Do we tell the pets not to make any noise?" Megala asked.

"No," Heiku said, smiling. "We just send for them all and spank them with no explanation."

"Everyone knows Iason's pet will win," Headmaster Sung declared. "He's certainly been spanked the most."

"What's the prize for winning?" Omaki asked.

Raoul smiled. "I have some party gifts set aside for just this sort of thing."

"Is this a bare-bottomed spanking?" Sanyara asked.

"Yes, yes. Let's see some skin," Lord Quiahtenon replied. "Make it an old-fashioned, over-the-knee spanking. No gloves."

"I don't have a pet tonight," Yutaku said, smiling, "so I'll just watch."

"Nor I," Aertis said.

"No, no. You can be the official game-masters. You'll tell us when to start and decide when each pet is out of the game, and declare the winner!"

"Very well, I suppose I could do that," Lord Iman said.

"I'd prefer to watch," Aertis said shyly.

"Is this the sort of thing you usually do at *your* parties, Omaki?" Norju asked curiously.

"Unfortunately, yes," Lord Sami answered, and the Blondies all laughed.

"But we should all make a toast to Raoul for his magnificent party, before we call for the pets," Omaki declared.

"To Raoul!" Everyone toasted, drinking the punch.

"That's odd," Sanyara said, turning aside to Lord Nu.

"What is?"

"The punch tastes…different. Better, actually."

"Perhaps it's a new batch," Kobin replied, shrugging.

The other Blondies were all talking very loudly, and no one heard this particular comment, though all of them—the Rebel Six anyway—noticed something strangely familiar about the punch, though none of them could put their finger on precisely what it was.

Meanwhile Yui and some of the other attendants had notified the pets that they were wanted upstairs.

"What, *all* of us?" Emerald said, voicing what all of them were thinking.

"Yes, all of you," Yui replied, smirking at Regiland.

"What for?" Riki demanded.

"A game, I think," Yui replied innocently.

The pets made their way upstairs, gravitating to the punch bowl, where they ate cookies and drank punch, waiting for the Blondies to make clear what they were there for.

"I think," Yutaku said loudly, "that all the pets are here. Pets, if you could please join your Masters, we shall begin."

"Begin what?" Riki demanded, striding toward Iason.

"Riki, take your pants down."

"Why?"

"Because I told you to."

190

"But what did I do?"

"I don't have to give a reckoning to you. Obey me, Riki."

All around him, the pets were engaged in similar conversations with their Masters, all of them seemingly oblivious to the fact that they were *all* going to be spanked, each one so focused on the humiliation of his or her own castigation.

Eventually all the pets were in position, though there was still a lot of fussing, and even some tears on the part of a few of the girls.

"They should be disqualified," Xian remarked, motioning to the girls.

"But we haven't even started yet," Yutaku replied.

"Pets!" Lord Quiahtenon bellowed. "You will be SILENT!"

The room was dead quiet.

"Now," Lord Iman said calmly, "we can begin. On your marks, get set, go!"

Thus commenced the spanking of the pets. Lord Faire's Emerald was disqualified almost immediately, followed by Jewel, the pet of Kobin. Next came Elisif, the Headmaster's pet. Ima, Heiku's pet, was the next to go.

Riki thought he was being spanked because of the D64-Reverse Modulator, and so he quietly endured his punishment, too humiliated to realize he was part of a game. Iason's hand was familiar, even comforting in a way, the firm slaps coming down on his rear in predictable intervals. He grit his teeth and winced, but did not make a sound.

Finally it was down to two pets: Riki and Golarian, Lord Kahn's pet. The Blondies began to cheer and call out names, depending on who they wanted to win, and at this point both pets realized they were part of some sick Blondie perversion party game.

But Riki, who had been bested by Golarian with Ima, was not about to be humiliated twice. He knew how to take punishment, and though Iason's hand burned like the blazes, he refused to capitulate.

Eventually Golarian could take no more of the infamous arm of Xanthus Kahn. He cried out miserably, and thus the competition came to an end.

So with cheers and toasts to Riki, Iason Mink was proclaimed the winner of the contest. Raoul brought a gift over to Iason, and handed it to him.

"Your prize," he said courteously.

Riki stood up, rubbing his ass. "You mean I don't get a prize?" he demanded. "I'm the one who got spanked!"

"Riki," Lord Mink admonished quickly.

"He has a point," Heiku admitted.

"Yes, give the poor pet a prize," Lord Sung suggested.

"Very well," Raoul agreed, fetching another present. He handed it to Riki, who, seeming rather surprised, took it.

"What do you say, Riki?" Iason prompted.

"Holy shit!" Riki replied.

The Blondies all laughed at this.

"I meant you were to *thank* Raoul," Lord Mink whispered, his face flushing red.

"Oh, sorry. Thanks, Lord Am."

Raoul bowed graciously.

"Well, open it!" someone called out.

Riki looked afraid to touch the handsomely-wrapped present, topped with a beautiful, sparkling bow. He gingerly removed the bow, looking as though he wanted to keep it.

The Blondies seemed amused at this, and at the way he slowly unwrapped the present without tearing the paper.

"Goodness, Iason. He acts like he's never gotten a present before," Kobin remarked.

Lord Mink frowned at this, and realized it was true. He didn't lavish Riki with gifts the way he should, especially since he knew the way he reacted to being given a gift.

"Well, finally. He's gotten to the box," Omaki reported, smiling.

Riki opened the box and stared at a sphere. "What is it?" he asked.

"I'll show you." Raoul turned the sphere on and it immediately levitated, pulsing through a full spectrum of colors.

"Oh, cool," Riki said with a smile.

"It will play music as well. It has an immense database stored in it. Try it."

Riki thought about it for a moment and then said, "Play *I Ain't Got Nobody But You* by the Icarian Harmonics."

The sphere immediately began playing a sultry tune that reminded him of Midas and the clubs there. The Blondies all clapped at his choice, apparently finding it sophisticated enough to meet their standards.

"Open your gift, Iason," Raoul pressed.

"Goodness, it wasn't really necessary," Iason said, opening the present gracefully but with less care than Riki had with his. It was a box of Aristian Red Emperor chocolates. Lord Mink was genuinely surprised. "I've never had these before."

"I know you haven't. They've just come onto the market. And I've heard they're absolutely delicious—and come with the same aphrodisiac propertics as the wine."

"You must have one. Everyone, pass the box around."

"We wouldn't dream of eating all your chocolates, Iason," Konami Sung laughed. "Take them home with you. We have plenty to eat here."

"Yes, Raoul, the hors d'oeuvres are absolutely delicious," Lord Nu said.

"And the punch is *especially* good," Headmaster Sung added. "I'm having my third cup now."

"Well, there's plenty more. Pets, you may return to your party room," Raoul announced.

The pets all left the room, looking a bit grumpy at the "game" they had been invited to partake in. As they made their way downstairs to the party room, they vocalized their thoughts about the game.

"That sucked," Riki declared, somehow expressing with those two meager words the entirety of the experience for all of them.

"At least *you* got a prize," Golarian complained. "I got my ass beat raw for nothing."

"Riki's used to it," Ima teased. "I've even seen him being spanked, right in front of me."

"Shut up, whore," Riki spat.

The girls all opened their mouths in horror.

"You can't call her that!" Jewel protested.

"Yes, Riki, that was rude," Elisif declared.

Ima put her hand to her mouth and ran off to one corner, crying.

"Ima," Riki called after her.

"Nice job, idiot," Katze said, punching him in the arm. "Wait until she tells her Master."

"She *is* a whore," Riki replied defensively. "She didn't even know the baby was mine until they proved it was."

"Even so, you can't call her that."

"Why is everyone against me?"

Katze put his hand on Riki's shoulder. "Let's go sit down."

"Fine. Or should I go talk to her and apologize?"

"Maybe that wouldn't be a bad idea," Katze agreed.

Riki sauntered toward the group of girls that had gathered around Ima. They turned and saw him, giving him nasty looks.

"Go away, Riki," Emerald snarled.

"Let me talk to her," Riki demanded.

"Why should we? You just called her a *whore*," Elisif replied.

"I'm sorry about that. I…sometimes I say things I don't really mean."

The girls were quiet at this, turning to Ima to see her reaction.

"I'll talk to him," she sniffed.

The girls backed away, leaving the two of them alone.

"Ima. I'm sorry about what I said," Riki began.

"It's all right. I shouldn't have teased you."

"I wish…things had worked out differently. Iason was going to let me keep the baby."

"Yeah? I'm sorry I lost it, Riki," Ima whispered.

"It's not *your* fault."

"I know. Riki?"

"Yeah?"

"Why couldn't you….?"

"Oh….*that*. Well, see, I had just come a few minutes before."

Ima frowned. "But your ring restrictions?"

"They're off for tonight."

"Oh. Then you're still attracted to me?"

Riki smiled. "Of course. You're still hot."

"You don't think I'm fat?"

"Hell, no."

"Riki?"

"Hmmm?"

"Do you think we'll ever be together again?"

"I don't know but...I kinda doubt it. I think I just blew my one chance with you, tonight."

"Golarian doesn't know how to fuck. It *hurt*."

Riki laughed at this. "Are you just saying that?"

Ima shook her head. "No. I had to *pretend* to come."

"No shit?"

"Yeah. It wasn't like it was...with you. Hey...do you have my barrette?"

Riki looked away for a moment. "Yeah. I have it."

"Oh, thank goodness! Master Heiku is ever so angry about it! He keeps spanking me for it!"

The mongrel reached into his pocket and took out the gamian barrette, holding it out to her.

She took it, smiling. "Why did you say you didn't have it?"

Riki shrugged. "I just wanted to keep something to remember you by."

"Oh." Ima took the barrette she was wearing out of her hair and handed it to him. "You can have this one. It doesn't have gamians in it. It's not worth anything—my Master won't notice it's gone."

"Thanks," Riki said, shoving it in his pocket. He eyed her see-thru top, feeling an erection coming on. "Well, I'd better go now."

"Why?"

"Because...you're kinda turning me on."

Ima giggled. "What if I take off my top?"

Riki blinked. "What?"

Ima unfastened her top and let it fall to the floor.

"Holy shit!"

"Let's have sex now, Riki," Ima purred.

The mongrel backed away. "No. I can't."

"Why not? I can see you're aroused."

"Because I'll get in trouble! We'll *both* be in big trouble!"

"Ima!" Emerald admonished. "Why did you just take your top off?"

"Because I feel sexy like this. Why don't you take off yours?"

Emerald, not the brightest of pets, and feeling suddenly extraordinarily aroused, shrugged. "Sure," she agreed, releasing her generous breasts from their restraints.

"Oh God," Riki whispered.

The next thing he knew, *all* the girls were stripping, and trying to take *his* shirt off.

"Have sex with *all* of us!" Elisif suggested.

"Yes, Riki!" Jewel squealed. "Fuck us."

"Um," Riki said, looking at Ima.

"Fuck me first," Ima declared.

"And then me," Elisif said.

"Then fuck me…*hard*," Jewel said.

"And then *me*," Emerald said.

"I want sex, too," Shima said, pouting.

Riki, surrounded by topless girls and finding himself extraordinarily aroused by their provocative invitations, was having trouble extricating himself from the situation. The girls had pulled his shirt up and were suckling his nipples. The next thing he knew, he was on the floor, and Ima was straddling him, unzipping his pants. Everywhere he looked he saw naked breasts—and sometimes even more than that. He groaned, feeling completely helpless.

Katze, however, could be counted on to remedy the situation. In the next instant he was at Riki's side, roughly pulling him to his feet.

"*What* are you doing?" he demanded.

"They're attacking me!" Riki complained.

"You didn't look like you were resisting much."

"They're half-naked! Some of them *completely* naked!"

The girls began trying to undress Katze, kissing his throat and licking him. He swatted them away like flies. He looked around the room and saw similar scenes going on everywhere—pets and attendants alike undressing, kissing, and groping.

"Something's wrong. Get out of here, Riki!" Katze said, pushing him towards the stairs.

MEANWHILE, UPSTAIRS, THE BLONDIES WERE ALL in an agitated state, though none of them (except, perhaps *one*) knew why.

"I don't know why, but those spankings aroused me," Lord Nu confessed, uncrossing his legs.

"Yes," Sanyara agreed. "It's very peculiar."

"I have an erection," Yousi announced.

Raoul frowned. Something about the scenario was decidedly *too* familiar.

Lord Quiahtenon looked at Yousi. "Come, Yousi. Let's find a room." He turned to Raoul. "Assuming you don't mind?"

"No, no," Lord Am said, puzzled. He looked at his punch glass, suspicious. "Iason, if I didn't know better, I'd say you'd been tampering with the punch."

Lord Mink looked equally bewildered. "But I haven't."

"Excuse me," Kobin said. "Would you mind if I begged for a room, also?"

"Might I join you?" Norju asked.

"Why, yes, actually," Lord Nu said. "I would be delighted."

At that moment, Riki came upstairs looking for Iason.

"What is it, Riki?" the Blondie asked, frowning.

"You wouldn't believe me if I told you. They're all taking off their clothes and having an orgy down there."

"What!" All the Blondies leapt to their feet and went racing down the stairs to the party room, with the exception of Iason and Omaki.

Omaki began laughing as though he'd just heard the funniest joke in the world.

Iason frowned. "What do you know about this, Omaki?"

The Blondie tried to stop laughing. "I put Tarnacsian cider in the punch," he confessed.

"You didn't!"

"I did."

"You're incorrigible," Iason scolded. He turned to Riki. "You were good to come upstairs, Riki."

"I just knew my ass couldn't take any more spankings."

"I'm sorry about the spanking. It was just a little party revelry."

"Oh yeah, that was great fun," Riki said sarcastically.

Iason rose. "Well, let's find a room."

"What do you mean?"

"I mean I had two glasses of that punch and I'm ready to burst. Only I haven't any idea where the rooms are."

"I'll show you," Omaki volunteered.

"Don't get any funny ideas," Iason warned. "I may be aroused, but I'm not desperate."

"Iason, I'm hurt," Lord Ghan said, holding his heart as though he had been mortally wounded. "That you would say that to *me*, after everything we've shared together?"

"Are we going to find a room, or not? I've got a boner you wouldn't believe," Riki remarked.

"This way," Omaki said, leading them down a hallway and up a spiral staircase. They came to the first room on the floor and entered it, finding it more than suitable for their needs.

"Wow, this place is really decked out," the mongrel declared.

"Riki, take off your clothes," Iason commanded.

Omaki stood in the doorway, leaning on the doorframe. "I'm willing to pay you to stay—just to watch, mind you."

"Omaki, close the door! Anyone could walk by!"

Lord Ghan, taking this as an invitation to stay, closed the door behind him.

Iason Mink was simply too aroused to even notice that the Blondie had invited himself into the room. He was tugging impatiently on his clothes, trying to get out of them as quickly as possible.

Omaki, deciding to make the most of the moment, undressed as well.

"Oh, Riki," Iason said, kissing him with wild enthusiasm. "I'm simply dying for you."

"Well, I hope they have some lube in here," Riki replied, a little less romantically.

"Try the drawers by the bed—those tables there," Omaki suggested.

"Omaki!" Iason exclaimed. "What are you doing in here?"

"What? You told me to close the door!"

"But I meant for you to be on the *other* side of the door—goodness, are you completely naked?"

"Yes, I am," Omaki said, walking toward him. "Do I look good?"

"I'm not looking," Iason said, shielding his eyes.

"Oh, come now, Iason, it's not like this is the *first* time we've seen each other naked," the Blondie teased.

Riki opened his eyes wide at this, but said nothing.

"What do you think, Riki? Am I not a god?"

"You're very sexy," Riki conceded.

"Riki," Iason protested, sounding hurt.

"I mean, he's nothing compared to you, but he *is* good-looking."

"I have an idea," Omaki said. "Why don't Riki and I both pleasure you, Iason. I'll take the back end, and he can take your cock."

"What do you mean by *take the back end?*" Riki demanded.

"I'll stick my tongue up his ass."

"Oh. Yeah. He likes that."

Iason, unable to help himself, groaned at this scenario.

"That's it," Omaki encouraged. "Why don't you just lie back on the bed and enjoy yourself?"

Iason Mink was not the sort of Blondie to make rash decisions. Especially when it came to sharing Riki. However, Tarnacsian cider had a very potent effect on him—and to make things worse, he had enjoyed a glass of Aristian Red Emperor wine in addition to trying out the chocolates—both of which were aphrodisiacs. Omaki's offer to stick his tongue up his ass while Riki pleasured him in other ways was, at that moment, simply too much to resist.

He found himself lying back on the bed, allowing Omaki to push his legs back to gain access to his portal, and hissed loudly when the Blondie began his ministrations.

Riki, for his part, straddled him backwards in order to service him, his ass close enough to Iason's face that the Blondie could offer him a few tantalizing licks with his tongue. The mongrel cried out loudly each time, and Iason tried to give some attention to his cock with his hand, but the truth of the matter was, he was so overcome with the pleasure he was being given that he was unable to offer much in return.

"Just relax," Riki suggested finally. "Give into the moment."

So that is exactly what Iason did. He writhed and moaned, feeling overwhelmed by the myriad sensations coursing through his body, and delighting in the view of the mongrel's ass. The cider had made him so anxious for sex that he honestly did not care that it was Omaki servicing him so sweetly in his nether regions. He knew Riki was loving him elsewhere, and that was all that mattered.

With a great sigh of contentment, he came, glorious waves of pleasure shooting through his loins as he arched his back, closing his eyes.

"Can I fuck you now?" Riki asked eagerly.

"Hold on now," Omaki said, rising up. "If you're going to fuck him, I get to fuck *you*."

"Yeah, okay," Riki agreed quickly.

Iason frowned. "I don't know how I feel about that."

"Then, what if I fuck you, Iason, and after that the mongrel can fuck me?" Omaki suggested.

Riki looked to Iason to see how he would respond to this scenario.

"Very well," Iason agreed, with a slight frown.

"Then keep your legs wide open," Omaki directed. "I'm fucking you just like this."

"Lubricate yourself first," Iason demanded.

"Oh. Right."

Omaki found some oil and poured a generous amount on his cock while Riki watched.

"This is hot," the mongrel proclaimed.

Omaki pressed his engorged organ up to Iason's portal. "I've dreamt of this moment for as long as I can remember," he confessed, sliding inside. "Oh, yes. What a grip! Magnificent!"

"You'll tell no one about this, Omaki," Iason warned.

"Hmmm? Oh, no, of course not. Oh, Iason!"

"Are you as tight as he is?" Riki asked suspiciously.

"Well, I make no guarantees about *that*," Omaki said, grinning. "If you prefer, I can suck you off."

Riki groaned, finding the waiting for his turn to be excruciating.

"I'm not going to last long, I'm afraid. Ah, you're squeezing me! Heavens! It's imminent now!" Lord Ghan said, fucking Iason for all he was worth. "Ah! I'm coming!"

"It's my turn," Riki announced.

"I'm still coming," Omaki protested. "*Ohhhhh!*"

"Okay, and I've changed my mind. I want *both* of you to service me."

"What do you want, love?" Iason asked softly.

"I want your tongue up my ass, and Omaki on his knees, giving me fellatio. But when I say it's time, I want him to turn around so I can fuck him."

"Dear God, that was heavenly," Omaki moaned.

"Did you hear the change of plan?" the mongrel asked impatiently.

"I heard."

"Well, everyone here has come except me. So I expect outstanding performances," the mongrel declared.

"Your bottom is still red from your spanking," Iason remarked, getting into position.

"Why am I not surprised about that? Lord Ghan? Are you getting up?"

"Yes, yes. Just give me a moment to enjoy my rapture."

"My cock is about to explode! I—*ohhhhhh!*" The mongrel's censure was cut short when Iason began to flick his tongue around his sphincter.

"Yes, I'm up. You want me on my knees, is that right?"

"Bah," Riki could only manage to say, his skills of articulation having been severely compromised by Iason's superb lingual arts.

"I'll take that as a *yes*." Omaki got up and knelt on the bed before Riki, taking him full in the mouth.

"Argh!" Riki gasped, allowing his hands to rest on Lord Ghan's head. His own head was spinning; he couldn't believe Iason was letting him be serviced by another Blondie, other than Raoul.

He wanted to last. He wanted to make it last forever. But the Tarnacsian cider, and the build-up of participating in a sex session with Omaki and Iason, and then watching Omaki with Iason, was too much.

"Huh!" he gasped, unable to even say the words *Holy Shit!*, so intense was his pleasure. He had been incapable of saving himself in order to fuck Omaki, and simply came in the Blondie's mouth.

Lord Ghan smiled at this, wiping his lips. "I take it I missed your cue."

"Oh shit," Riki breathed, "that was incredible."

"Well, as long as everyone is satisfied."

At that moment there came a pounding at the door.

"Who's in there?" Raoul demanded.

"Come in," Omaki said mischievously.

"Omaki!" Iason gasped, reaching for the comforter to cover himself.

Raoul opened the door, took in the scene, and then pointed at Omaki. "You," he said, heading menacingly toward him.

"What?" Lord Ghan laughed, shielding himself with a pillow.

"What did you do to my punch? You put Tarnacsian cider in it, didn't you?"

"Well, I might have put just a *pinch* in it," Omaki admitted.

"How *dare* you!"

"You should be thanking me!"

"Why should I be thanking you? You just *ruined* my party!"

"Now, calm down. I hardly *ruined* your party. Now it will be a party everyone really remembers."

Raoul, at this point, seemed to finally *fully* digest the scene that was before him. He helped Omaki to his feet and shoved him roughly out the door, closing it behind him.

"But I haven't any clothes on!" Omaki protested, from the hall.

Raoul locked the door. He was shaking, both from the Tarnacsian cider and the sight of Iason lying naked in bed.

"We just had sex," Riki informed him. "So we're kinda spent."

Raoul eyed Iason's newly-forming erection, which was not completely hidden from view, and smiled.

RAOUL'S PARTY GENERATED INTO COMPLETE CHAOS. ONCE the Blondies apprehended the pets fornicating downstairs, there was a second administration of spankings, with some chasing scenes thrown in, but not long after this the Blondies abandoned their pets to their own pursuits as they went off in search of carnal pleasures.

Nearly everyone who came paired off with someone—Lord Quiahtenon with Yousi, Headmaster Sung with Aertis, Kobin with Norju. Lord Ven was with Omaki, who had walked naked into the great hall, while Xanthus chose Lord Zavi. Elusiax was with Yutaku, Lord Sami sought out Juthian, Raoul was with Iason and Riki, and Megala Chi was nowhere to be found.

All the while the orchestra played elegant music in the corner of the great hall, which was completely incongruent with the running about that went on, and the various knocking over of chairs, and the broken vases (thankfully not Vergattis) that cluttered the floor, almost as if Raoul was determined to have his refined party anyway, and that simply by playing the right music, he could achieve the effect he wanted.

At long last the effects of the Tarnacsian cider began to wear off, and the Blondies gathered again in the great hall, famished.

"This would be a good time for dinner," Raoul announced, "if I can find any attendants."

"I can't get out of this chair," Kobin Nu said.

"Me either," Sanyara agreed.

"I'll go see if I can find someone to help, Master," Yui volunteered. He was, in truth, a little afraid to go down to the party room, as the last time he had gone there it had been a sight to behold—naked pets and attendants everywhere, and fornication that made his eyeballs nearly fall out. The spankings administered by the Blondies did little to mitigate the effects of the Tarnacsian cider, and as soon as they had left the pets and attendants had gone back to whatever they were doing.

But he went down there now, and found the place quite a different scene. Most of the pets and attendants were dressed—though some of the clothing was inside out—and they had all gathered around the empty trays of appetizers, looking forlorn.

"I need someone to help me serve the Blondies," Yui announced.

"What about us?" Riki demanded. He was miffed at being sent by Iason back down to the party room, after everything he had done with Omaki, first, and then Raoul. "I'm starving."

"I'm sorry, Riki, you'll have to wait. The Blondies come first."

"We'll help." Ru and Kahlan got up, as did Tai and Toma, Katze, Daryl, and Sarius, and several of the other attendants.

"Thank you. They're in bad shape, upstairs," Yui reported.

"*They're* in bad shape," Riki laughed. "I can't even feel my dick."

"Where did you go, Riki?" Katze asked.

"You wouldn't believe me if I told you."

"You'll tell us, before the night is through."

Riki only laughed, shaking his head.

The attendants managed to make their way upstairs.

"Ah! We have attendants," Raoul exclaimed, seeming profoundly relieved. "We can adjourn to the table."

"You know, we could have eaten without attendants," Yutaku said thoughtfully.

"What?! How barbaric," Raoul said, rising. He pulled Yui aside.

"Yes, Master?"

"I need you to take care of another matter, when you're done serving."

"Yes?"

"The rooms upstairs may have been…compromised. Please see that the beds are all made with fresh sheets."

Yui stared at him for a moment, calculating how much work that would be. Then he obediently inclined his head. "Of course, Master."

"You may require some assistance. Don't hesitate to ask for it. The other attendants should help you."

"Yes, Master. Thank you."

Yui turned, trying to hide his emotions. He was tired and he was hungry. And it had not escaped him that Raoul had been in the same room as Iason Mink. And now he was to take care of all the bedding, which had already been done once that day, on top of serving the meal? How many rooms were they talking about?

"Is something wrong, Yui?" Ru asked, looking worried.

"No. I mean…yes, but, there's nothing I can do about it."

"Is there anything I can do to help?"

Yui looked at Ru, his eyes filling with tears. "Yes, actually. You can help me with the rooms after we're done serving. Master Raoul says all the beds need new sheets."

"I'll help. And the others will help, too."

"But you're hungry, surely."

"I am, but we can help you first."

"And then we have to feed the pets…."

"It'll be okay," Ru said in a comforting way. "Why don't you take a few moments to compose yourself? Slip into the kitchen, grab something to eat, and just sit down for a few minutes."

"Are you sure?" Yui asked, eyes wide.

"I'm sure. We've got this covered."

"Thank you, Ru."

Yui did as instructed, taking a much-needed break, while the others brought all the warming-domes to the table, along with the wine.

The Blondies were in high spirits, now that food was imminent. They laughed about nothing in particular, seeming to have some sort of private joke among themselves.

Katze lit the candles on the table, giving the room a nice ambiance.

"Raoul, your villa is splendid," Lord Nu declared.

"Hear, hear!" the other Blondies cried out, raising their wine glasses in a toast.

"I thank you," Raoul said, with a slight incline of his head. "But it's Megala and Katan you should be toasting. They are the ones who designed this masterpiece."

"To Megala and Katan!" Omaki said, raising his glass.

"Megala and Katan!" the others all toasted.

"And who do we have to thank for whatever was in the punch?" Norju asked, eliciting a few laughs.

"That would be Omaki," Raoul said, seeming more than slightly unhappy.

"To Omaki, then!" Lord Faire toasted.

"Omaki!" everyone repeated, except Lord Am, who looked disgusted, and Iason, who was flushed pink.

"I do believe this is the best party I've ever been to," Konami Sung stated.

"We're not surprised to hear *that*. Is this the best party *you've* ever been to, Aertis?" Xian quipped, and some of the Blondies laughed, while the others looked puzzled.

"Oh yes," Aertis answered innocently.

Konami reddened, pretending to look at something on the wall.

Omaki snorted.

"So who did *you* pair up with, Raoul?" Heiku asked.

"As if you have to ask *that*," Xian replied, arching a brow.

"Oh, really?" Lord Quiahtenon looked toward Iason, who was blushing furiously.

"Then this really *is* the best party ever, just like the good old days," Megala Chi said happily.

"Where were *you*, Megala?" Xian asked suspiciously.

"Hmmm? Oh, nowhere, in particular."

"You had to be *somewhere*."

"How carefully did you look at those blueprints, Raoul?" Omaki demanded.

Raoul opened his mouth and then shut it, giving Megala a questioning look.

"Oh, no," Megala said, putting his hands up. "Really. I wouldn't dream of it."

"Hmmm."

"Let's eat, shall we?" Yutaku suggested.

"A splendid idea," Lord Sung agreed, taking the lid off one of the warming domes. "I'm so famished I can barely think."

The Blondies dug in, heaping food onto their plates, while the attendants stood by, ready to pour more wine. The main course was broiled lamb which was cooked so tender the meat fell from the bones. Of course, there was all manner of side dishes—corn, mashed potatoes and gravy, galamati roots, cheese-drenched noodles, and a fresh salad. And for dessert, there was a chocolate-covered caramel pudding—and in one of the dessert dishes—Raoul informed them, was a prize—Elusiax Kain found it in his: it was a ring, and a very expensive one, with an emerald on it and a special band that adjusted permanently to the size of the first finger it was put on—Xeronian technology, of course, accomplished that. After it was washed off, Elusiax was most pleased with his prize and commented several times that he had never been to a better party in his life, that the ring was spectacular, and that the games had been especially enjoyable.

"We only played *one* game, Elusiax," Xian pointed out.

"Only one? But I thought...." Now Elusiax's voice trailed off as he gave Yutaku a questioning look.

Lord Iman blushed, for the truth of the matter was that he only persuaded Elusiax to join him in one of the rooms after convincing him it was one of Heiku's games. Once they were inside the room, Elusiax proved that, although he was an upstanding Elite in all respects, he was subject to the same temptations as everyone else, when it came to consuming Tarnacsian cider.

"Perhaps we should play *another* game, after this," Heiku said joyfully.

The Blondies all groaned.

"We don't want to play one of your games, Ku-ku," Xian teased.

Lord Quiahtenon frowned. "Don't call me that."

"He doesn't like to be called Ku-ku," Yousi confirmed.

This, of course, set off a long stream of name-calling, every Blondie feeling compelled, for some reason, to call Heiku by the unwanted appellation.

The attendants tried hard not to laugh or smile during all this, though the teasing of Lord Quiahtenon pushed them to their limits.

"But I have in mind a *splendid* game," Heiku said, raising his hands as if to ward off a swarm of bees.

"I don't think our pets cared much for the *last* game," Kobin remarked.

"This one doesn't involve the pets."

"What is it, then?" Norju asked.

"It's called Spill or Speculate. Each one of us has to spill about the details of our pairing this evening, or else confess as to who we'd *like* to pair with."

"I'm not playing," Iason declared.

"Nor I," Raoul agreed.

"Of course you're playing! Everyone is playing."

"How does one win, exactly?" Xian demanded.

"We all vote on who gave the most salacious answer."

"Does the winner get a prize?" Lord Nu asked.

Everyone looked to Raoul.

"Well, I suppose I *do* have something set aside yet for this sort of thing," he admitted. "But I'm not playing."

"You have to play. The penalty for not playing is ten strikes with a paddle."

"What! That's barbaric!" Raoul exclaimed.

"Those are the rules."

Xanthus Khan started laughing, and his laugh proved infectious; soon all the Blondies were laughing.

"So! Shall we begin?"

"We're in the middle of dinner," Raoul protested.

"I don't see why we can't start the game," Kobin Nu said. "But I think we should start with *you*, Ku-ku. Spill or Speculate."

Heiku ignored the nickname and, much to everyone's surprise, began to give more details about his encounter with Yousi than anyone wanted to hear.

"Stop," Lord Faire pleaded, putting his hands to his ears. "I think I've heard enough."

"Yes, we've all heard enough," Xian agreed. "Who's next?"

"Let's move to the left. That would be you, Kobin. Spill or Speculate!"

Lord Nu thought about this for a moment, taking a drink of his wine. "I've always wanted to pair with Gideon Lagat."

The Blondies made a clamor at this, much to Kobin's mortification.

"All right, all right. He's given his answer," Raoul said, trying to calm everyone down. "Norju?"

Norju seemed to take his cue from Kobin. "I suppose I'd pair with Orphe Zavi."

This caused another commotion, everyone turning to Katan Zavi for his reaction.

"I'll be sure to tell my brother," Katan said, winking at Norju.

"You wouldn't," Lord Faire said, looking horrified.

"Now, now, one of the rules is that all of this stays in this room," Heiku announced.

"You didn't specify that before," Xian remarked.

"Well, I'm saying it now."

"I agree," Raoul said, nodding. "This stays here. I wouldn't want any of this ending up on The Channel. And that goes for *everything* that's happened at this party."

"Agreed," Konami Sung said quickly.

The rest of the Blondies also agreed, much to Raoul's relief.

"Who's next?" Heiku said merrily.

"It's Headmaster Sung," Raoul said.

Lord Sung looked decidedly uncomfortable. "I'll take the ten."

"What!" Everyone cried in unison.

The Headmaster nodded, rising. "Yes, I'd rather take the paddle, than answer either of those questions."

"But Headmaster, we all *know* who you've been with," Xian teased.

At this, Aertis Jin looked extraordinarily guilty, but some of the other Blondies seemed puzzled.

Xanthus stood up. "If he said he's taking the ten, let him take them. I'll administer them. Have you a paddle?"

Raoul rose, looking around for Yui. "Yui!" he called.

Yui came running in from the kitchen.

"Bring me a paddle. A big one."

"Yes, Master," Yui said, looking frightened.

Raoul saw his look and wanted to reassure him, but felt he couldn't in front of everyone watching. So he simply waited until Yui returned with the paddle. "Very good. You may go," he said quietly.

Relieved, Yui backed away.

Raoul tossed the paddle to Xanthus, who caught it admirably with one hand.

"All right, Konami. Stand behind your chair, hands on the chair," Xanthus commanded.

The Blondies whistled and cheered as Xanthus flipped the paddle around in the air a few times, and then brought it towards the Headmaster's rear end, as though practicing his swing.

Then, he struck. "One!" Everyone yelled.

*WHACK!*

"Two!"

*WHACK!*

"Three!"

The Blondies counted all the way to ten, and Konami, for his part, took his blows stoically, though he winced and closed his eyes for the last few. He sat down gingerly, looking decidedly unhappy about the game.

"Who's next?" Yousi cried out joyfully.

"It's Iason," Raoul said, frowning.

Lord Mink took a sip of his wine, considering. "I suppose I've always wanted to pair with…Commander Voshka Khosi," he said finally.

"That shouldn't count," Xian protested. "Everyone knows he's already slept with Vosh."

"What! You slept with Commander Khosi?" Katan Zavi said with surprise.

"You didn't specify in the rules it had to be someone we've never slept with," Iason replied.

"That's true, you didn't," Raoul said, coming to Iason's defense.

"Well that should have been a *given*," Heiku complained. "Iason, you have to pick someone else."

The other Blondies agreed, and so Lord Mink took another drink of his wine, avoiding the gaze of both Raoul and Omaki. "Very well. I suppose I've always wanted to sleep with…Yenna."

"Yenna? Who's Yenna?" Lord Nu demanded.

"Yenna was one of Iason's pets," Lord Sung clarified.

This elicited such a loud reaction from the Blondies that Raoul was forced to stand up, asking them to calm down.

"All right, all right, he's given his answer."

"Yutaku is next," Yousi announced.

Lord Iman dared a glance at Elusiax, and, finding the man looking rather stiff around the mouth, decided not to relate the details of their congress. "I've always wanted to sleep with the Headmaster," he admitted.

As one might imagine, the hall erupted with this announcement. Headmaster Sung's face went red as an Aristian beet, and Aertis Jin frowned with jealousy.

Raoul was next. "I had sex with Iason, and I'm not ashamed to admit it," he declared.

"Raoul," Iason hissed.

The Blondies all pounded their fists on the table with this pronouncement. "Details, details, details!" they demanded in unison.

"I gave him fellatio, and then I penetrated him," Raoul said, giving Iason an apologetic look.

Iason, for his part, looked furious.

"Now it's Aertis Jin's turn," Yousi said happily.

Aertis was in a bind. If he opted out and took the ten strikes, everyone would guess he had been with the Headmaster. And he couldn't actually say he had been with the Blondie, so he had one option left. And he knew that the confession would make Konami jealous. "I suppose," he said slowly, "I've always wanted to have sex with Eludius Ren."

"Who is that?" Xian asked, and everyone else wondered the same.

"Eludius Ren is a fourth-year at the Academy," Konami Sung said through clenched teeth.

Omaki arched a brow, sensing the tension between Konami and Aertis.

Sanyara Ven was next, and he related his encounter with Omaki in full detail.

Next it was Lord Khan, who had paired with Katan Zavi, but rather than disclose the details of that congress, he chose to name Zanbar Su as the Blondie he most wanted to sleep with.

"Zanbar Su, from The Channel?" Xian demanded.

"Of course Zanbar Su from The Channel. How many Zanbar Sus can there be?" Heiku retorted.

"Now it's Katan Zavi's turn," Yousi announced.

"I'll admit it. I've always wanted to sleep with Iason Mink," Katan said.

Lord Mink blushed furiously at this as the Blondies all roared with laughter.

"Now it's *my* turn," Yousi said.

"We don't want to hear *this* again," Xian sighed.

"I was going to say, that I always wanted to sleep with Aisha Rosen, but I can't remember who that is, now."

Heiku frowned at this.

"Aisha Rosen?" Megala said excitedly. "That's a very good choice."

"I doubt Aisha would enjoy being eyed by a simpleton," Lord Nu remarked with a smirk.

Heiku stood up, waving his bionic arm in a frightening manner, the hand and digits spinning in all different directions. "He's not a simpleton! In his day he had more wits about him than *all* of you put together! I'll not have you making disparaging remarks about him when I'm standing right here!"

"Heiku, sit down," Raoul admonished gently. "Kobin didn't mean it like he said it. Everyone knows Yousi was brilliant once."

"I'll have you know he's not as simple as you think! He *knows* you cheat him at the fish market, Kobin!" Heiku said, finally sitting down.

Kobin looked genuinely surprised at this, darkening a few shades.

"What about *you*, Megala? Are you going to tell us what you were up to this afternoon? Or do you choose Aisha Rosen, too?" Omaki asked.

"We *all* know who he's always wanted to sleep with," Xian drawled, and everyone laughed.

Megala blushed, and dared a fearful glance toward Raoul.

"I think I've had about enough of this game," Raoul sighed.

"Wait! He has to *say* it," Lord Quiahtenon declared.

"I admit…I've always wanted to sleep with Raoul," Megala said softly.

"What a big surprise," Xian quipped.

"Xian, you're next. Spill or Speculate," Heiku directed.

"Well," Lord Sami said, glancing nervously at the Headmaster, "I suppose I always wanted to sleep with…Yousi—back in the old days, of course."

Heiku spun his robotic fist menacingly. "Come near him now and I'll stuff this up your ass."

Xian held up his hands as if surrendering. "I wouldn't dream of it."

"Omaki, you're last. What do you have to say?"

Iason looked at the Blondie anxiously. Omaki, catching his eye, gave him a wink.

"Sanyara has already related the details of my afternoon. So I'll just say I've always wanted to sleep with Xanthus."

Lord Khan was so surprised that it looked like he might fall over.

All the Blondies cheered and whistled at this.

"Wait a minute! Elusiax hasn't gone yet!" Xian pointed out.

"Oh, must I go?" Elusiax asked.

"Yes, yes, we've all gone, now it's your turn," Heiku said impatiently. So Spill or Speculate."

"Well, I suppose I will confess that I had a most pleasant encounter this afternoon with…with…Yutaku Iman."

The Blondies all pressed him for details, which he gave reluctantly, consisting of his being rimmed by Yutaku and then afterwards fucked, with both of them coming so hard they screamed and scared the birds off the windowsill.

The Blondies were quiet for a moment.

"I say Elusiax wins," Heiku declared.

The others nodded. "Elusiax! Elusiax!" they chanted.

"Have we a prize?" Lord Nu asked.

"Yes, yes. I'll retrieve it." Raoul rose from his chair and returned with a wrapped gift. It turned out to be a grand chalice made of gold.

"Heavens," Sir Kain muttered. "This must have cost a fortune!"

"And every time you look at it, you'll think of those birds," Kobin quipped, and the Blondies all laughed.

"Gentlemen, it has been a pleasure," Headmaster Sung said, rising.

"What, don't tell me you're leaving? I thought you'd all stay the night?" Raoul protested.

"No, no. I'm afraid I have....certain obligations," Lord Sung replied.

The others began to rise, as well.

"It was a most *excellent* party," Kobin declared.

"Hear, hear!" the other Blondies said in unison.

"Well, as long as everyone had a good time," Raoul said, looking a little put out.

"We had a wonderful time, the food was delicious, and the company was perfect," Omaki assured him.

"Do you suppose our pets had a chance to eat?" Kobin remarked.

"Perhaps not," Raoul said, looking toward the attendants, who were still standing at attention, wine bottles in hand.

"Then perhaps we ought to let them eat first, before we go," Kobin suggested.

"An excellent idea," Raoul agreed happily.

The Blondies sat back down.

"And I have just the idea for a little game we can play, while we wait," Heiku announced.

The Blondies all groaned again.

# EPILOGUE

The day finally came for the new Orphanage to open in Midas, and Riki was so excited he could hardly finish his breakfast.

"Can we go now?" he asked, watching impatiently as Iason drank his coffee.

The Blondie smiled indulgently. "Make sure Ios has plenty of food. We won't be back until tonight."

"I'll watch after him, Riki," Tai promised.

"Thanks," the mongrel said, turning back to Iason. "Can we take my car?"

"I suppose," Iason agreed.

The Grand Opening of the Orphanage was a big event, and even though they arrived in Midas early, the place was already crowded. Riki, however, parked right in the front of the Orphanage in the VIP parking place especially for Riki the Dark. The bodyguards pulled in beside them, in the place reserved for Iason.

"Before we get out of the car, I have another surprise for you," Lord Mink said.

"Oh yeah?"

"Yes. You're sure they can't see through these windows?" The Blondie nodded to the crowd of children who were running toward the vehicle.

"Yeah, I'm sure. They're mirror windows, remember? We can see out but all they see are mirrors."

"In that case...." Lord Mink began unbuttoning his tunic.

"What are you doing?" Riki asked, bewildered.

"You'll see, in just a moment," the Blondie answered.

After he had unfastened his tunic a ways, he pulled it open, revealing his chest and his nipples—one of them pierced.

Riki stared in disbelief. "You did it…you really did it! You got your nipple pierced…for me?"

"Yes," Iason agreed. "For you."

"I can't believe it! Is it sore?"

"No. I opted for Acceleration."

"I should have guessed," Riki replied, grinning. "That means we can play tonight!"

"Oh? What did you have in mind?"

"You can be *my* pet."

"If that pleases you, Master," the Blondie purred, playing along.

"I can't *wait* until tonight!"

"We'd better get out of the car now," Iason said, buttoning up his tunic.

Children had gathered around the vehicle, pressing their faces against the windows in an attempt to see inside.

"They're cute," Riki laughed. "I guess it's your fan club."

Lord Mink smiled but said nothing.

They got out of the car and Riki was surprised when the children gathered, not around Iason, as he had expected, but around *him*—trying to hold his hands.

"What's this?" he asked, looking toward the Blondie in surprise.

Iason nodded ahead. "Take a look."

Riki looked and then did a double-take. In front of the Orphanage was a statue, but not a statue of Iason, as he would have expected. No, the statue was of *him*.

"What the fuck?" he said.

The children giggled at his use of profanity.

"Riki," Iason sighed.

"I mean—what is this? It's me! It's a statue of me!"

"It's your Orphanage, isn't it?"

"But I thought...."

"Go read the inscription," Iason suggested.

At the base of the statue were the words, in big, bold, letters: Riki the Dark. Under that was the inscription: *The famous mongrel who made this Orphanage possible and who believes that no child should be on the streets of Midas.*

Indeed, though Lord Mink had planned and financed every aspect of the Orphanage, he was determined not to take credit for it. This was Riki's Orphanage, and that was what the sign said over the entrance to it. All the children knew it, and so it was Riki that they wanted especially to see.

The Grand Opening had attracted crowds not only from Midas but from Tanagura—Elites that were curious about a fantastic project financed by Iason Mink.

And Riki's Orphanage *was* a fantastic enterprise. The hotel was only part of the Orphanage. Every child had his or her own luxurious room with facilities. But the real attraction had been built by Megala Chi, and consisted of a building unlike any other, filled with colorful tunnels, slides, ladders, swings, trampolines, bounce rooms, spaces filled with myriad balls, game rooms, secret passageways, a library, a school, an art studio, an infirmary, a kitchen and a great hall for eating, and a petting zoo. Beyond this there was a separate area which showcased rides, including a magnificent musical carousel with moving horses and creatures of all sorts, a train, bumper cars, an octopus ride, a house of mirrors, a haunted house ride, a water slide, and a roller coaster that turned upside-down. The carnival area also served sweets like frozen creams and dogs-on-a-stick, which, like the tickets for the rides, could be purchased with "good behavior" coins the children earned during the day at the Orphanage.

Riki's Orphanage was hailed as a great success. Several children were adopted that very day, in fact, by visitors who had come to see the attraction, including one little girl who was adopted by a Blondie—Yutaku Iman, to be precise, who was known for his unorthodox views on nearly everything. For a Blondie to take home a mongrel orphan child was the talk of the day, and everyone wondered what would happen to her, once she was enrolled in the Academy.

The Orphanage took in 407 children, and though that was a good number, both Riki and Iason knew that they still had work ahead of them, if they were truly going to reach every child on the streets of Midas.

Riki was in high spirits that day. He was practically worshiped by the children of the Orphanage, who all knew that he was responsible for the tremendous change in their standard of living. To go from living on the streets to staying at a place like Riki's Orphanage was such a drastic change that most of the children were practically giddy. They laughed and sang songs about Riki, including this one:


*Riki the Dark, Riki the Dark*
*He took us off of the street*
*Riki the Dark, Riki the Dark*
*He made us like the Elite!*


Although Riki frowned when he heard the song, he was nevertheless touched by the children's gratitude. It was good to see them happy, being fed and dressed in clean clothes. And Iason had outdone himself, when it came to the Orphanage. Riki couldn't have even imagined such a facility, if he had tried.

They were at the Orphanage all day. As night fell, fireworks were set off. The children screamed and applauded as the beautiful lights scattered across the sky.

Riki and Iason sat together near Riki's statue, watching. As they were sitting there, a bird came along and, with ambivalent precision, deposited his lifeforce on Riki's statue.

"Hey! A bird just crapped on my statue!" the mongrel complained.

Odi, who had been guarding them the whole day, laughed.

As if on cue, a robotic assistant rolled over to the statue and rectified the defaced area.

"Did you see that?" Riki exclaimed. "That robot just cleaned up that shit!"

"I saw," Iason said, smiling.

"This was an awesome day," Riki proclaimed.

"I'm glad you're happy about it."

"I *am* happy. This means so much to me. You did a great job with the Orphanage, Iason. I couldn't have asked for anything better. I don't know how you pulled it all off, but it's amazing."

Lord Mink smiled, nodding.

"And I love love *love* that you pierced your nipple for me," the mongrel continued in a lower voice. "I can't wait until tonight. Can I really be the Master?"

"Riki, where my heart is concerned, you're *always* the Master," the Blondie replied softly.

"Really?" the mongrel said, his eyes shining impishly. "Then, can I use a whip?"

**This Concludes *Taming Riki*, Volume II**

**The Saga Continues in *Taming Riki*, Volume III: *Alpha Zen***

Made in United States
Troutdale, OR
06/03/2023

10394782R00128